Retribution: A Novel
By
Tammy E. Shelley

Chapter One
2000
Chicago

"Well, what did you find out?" Angie exhaled her cigarette smoke with every word; then snubbed the half-smoked butt out with frustration. He wasn't answering fast enough. "Well?"

The raven-haired man leaned over, pulled a fat folder of documents out of his satchel, and dropped it on the table. The sound rang with finality. "It's all here." They both looked at the folder. "You're not going to like it. If I were you, I would just drop…"

Angie noticed that customers around them twisted in their seats to see if there was something to see, as if they could sense the apprehension and fervor in his voice. She thought about how their conversation, serious and probably life-changing, was a paradox to the usual buzz of radiant energy at the outdoor café.

She caught the spark in people's eyes when they saw Peter. He was her best friend from college who could stop a room with his rugged rock star makes-you-think-you-should-know-him good looks. She felt like the antithesis of Peter; average looks, average everything, but she had long ago accepted her qualities, and his. Angie tuned out the inquiring energies and thumping libidos around them as she opened the folder. Peter was talking to her, but she wasn't listening anymore.

She scanned the contents of the folder – looking for answers about who she was and who her mother was. The first document. A death certificate. Annabelle Mason. Died of heart failure at age 34. No complications. No autopsy. It was signed by a doctor whose name she could not read and by J. S. Snellin, Director of Iron Rope Sanatorium. *"My mother *was* there."* Angie didn't realize she had spoken aloud.

"Yes, yes, that's what I've been saying. Listen, I think we should just let this rest and marinate for a bit. You have a lot going on right now."

Angie looked up at her longtime friend. His brown eyes were framed with eyelashes that made girls jealous. His eyes reflected panic, concern and what was that other emotion – fear or worry? She couldn't tell. It was difficult not to be mesmerized by those eyes. She smiled, trying to ease her resting bitch face, closed the folder, and lit another cigarette.

"Oh no, I'm going to find out what happened to her. I have to know." What if it happens to me? That sobering thought dug in deeper and grew a few more roots. She caught the eye of their approaching server who seemed to sense that this was an intense meeting and turned on her heel in one swift movement to work on another table. Angie flicked the sooty ash impatiently in the ashtray, watching the retreating server. She inhaled deeply and turned to challenge her good looking best friend.

He leaned in to offer some privacy, "Angie. There are treatments now – better than back then – no electroshock or lobotomy; no primitive stuff. You're opening information that I just don't think you need to be worried about right now."

She pulled defiantly from her cigarette. "So, you think I can't handle this?" Her eyes motioned to the folder.

"No, I really don't think you can. I'm sorry, but as your very best friend, I have to say this. You are in for some pain. You have a great, promising career going here. How many times have you said that you wanted out of the restaurant business?" Angie watched him stir his green tea, a stall tactic she knew all too well. He was gathering arguments.

"You could be the next great American author. You won that one writing contest," his voice trailed off. "I just think you need to concentrate on your writing. This stuff can wait. It's not going anywhere." He wasn't meeting her eyes. It only made her more curious as to what the folder held and why he was so apprehensive about continuing on.

He took a sip of his sweet iced tea and sat back with an attitude of frustration that warned her that he wasn't kidding. She knew him; knew his mannerisms, his strengths and weaknesses, his dreams and goals, probably better than he knew himself.

"You're telling me that what's in this folder is worse than my blackouts, worse than the dreams, worse than the voices? I've been looking for her my whole life. This is more important than fixing restaurants or writing a story. This is real. I don't have a choice. I can't wait."

He dropped his head and shoulders in submission.

She hated to see him dejected and disappointed. "Listen, I will take these, read through them and call you in the morning. Peter. You've been great, but I have to do this." She flashed her best reassuring smile, with that little bit of – I dare you to stop me edge – grabbed the folder, and started to fumble in her purse.

Peter stopped her; his gentle touch on her arm. "No, I got this. You be careful and make sure you call."

Half smiling, she took up the fat folder. "Thank you for doing this." They stood and hugged. "I'll be fine. Really."

"Please keep me updated."

"I will."

She walked with a new sense of purpose down the city street. There was a sweet scent of freedom and possibility in the air, which she inhaled gratefully. She was on her way to finding answers to her nagging questions about her birth mother and her past, and how it may link to her mental issues.

Angie looked back. She could see Peter's silhouette sitting at the small table. He was her only close friend; this project of finding her mother has been a re-bonding time for them both. In college, they were inseparable. Then she met a guy and he met a guy and they each went on their own ways for a year. Now they were both single. Their lives ran in strange parallel lines.

She climbed the three flights of stairs wheezing, which reminded her that she wanted another cigarette. It aggravated her when the landlord said she couldn't smoke in the hallways anymore.

Her district manager found this place for her seven months ago. It was perfect at first; full of old-world charm, ancient fixtures, and claw-footed bathtubs. Then the honeymoon wore off. The neighbors were odd, mean, and standoffish, which was fine with her because she could be the same. But the neighbor directly below her surpassed even her level of bitchyness.

She scowled at a note, scribbled, and taped to the door of her third level studio apartment. She didn't need to open it; she knew what it said. It was an ongoing war with that neighbor underneath who complained at least once a week about the noise above.

She tossed the note aside as she entered her small apartment. *He was insane*, the neighbor below. She worked in the restaurant business, she wasn't ever home, the noise that he was complaining about was not her, but no matter how many times she tried to explain the situation, he continued to blame her. "What an ass hat," she muttered as she kicked off her flats.

Her apartment was a part of an old 100-year-old building unit in an upscale historic area of Naperville, Illinois. She pressed the lights on. The housing unit wasn't quite up to code and she suspected the electrical system was protected by some obscure set of Historical Society rules.

She dropped her purse on the faded cloth chair. Her curiosity won, and she picked the crumpled note up from the floor. The scrawl was unmistakable.

> Miss Simpson. You will stop the noise. If it starts up tonight, I will call the police. You are warned.
>
> Mr. Willis, Apt 3

She had no idea what he was talking about. Crumpling up the note, she recalled her actions from the previous night.

She had crawled up the horrid flights of stairs at around 11 p.m. She walked into her sparsely furnished apartment, showered and went to bed. No matter how much she tried to explain her schedule to him, it was of no use. It was times like these that she was glad she was a traveling advisor. At most, she stayed in one place six months, and usually the time was shorter. She was looking forward to the relocation from this particular job. The time was past due.

She faced the full-length mirror, uncovered it, and gazed at herself with all the answers reflected and unreadable in front of her. Was her mother a medium to chunky build? Or was she light and lithe? Did they have the same eyes? Did her mother also suffer from voices, dreams, and seizures? Did she have the same type of thick, straight hair; blonde with dark undertones? The woman of average height and weight looked back at her. Her hair was swept back into a bun. It was the only hairstyle that worked for her hair since it wasn't curly and it wasn't straight. And in the restaurant business, hair up and back is the rule.

She knew that her unremarkable features helped her blend in when she had to do mystery visits to restaurants. She was excellent at her job. Large restaurant chains paid copious amounts of money for her to come work out various problems – everything from employee moral to totally reorganizing the restaurant itself. She was like the hero of *Kitchen Nightmares*, without the star factor, but not without the attitude. But she really wanted to write. When she won a small, yet prestigious writing contest, it was a turning point – a moment of 'I guess I can do this.' For her, writing wasn't about survival and money. She had no children or spouse, not even a pet. Writing helped her work out her demons and her dreams. She needed to write to keep her sanity. Her journals kept her grounded.

However, she was usually exhausted and drenched in food grease and sweat; the thought of writing for publication was pushed far back into the list of things that must get done. It was a leap of faith to walk away from a steady paycheck.

She hoped that her mother was like her as she replaced the covering over the mirror (she believed it helped to keep the voices out). She walked over to the well-worn antique mahogany desk and sat with the fat envelope.

The room consisted of an over large cloth chair, one desk, one clunky, noisy fridge, a stove that only had one working burner, one twin size bed, and the mirror. In her job, there was no time to gather anything more than the necessities of life: cigarettes, water, and whatever leftover carry-out food that was still sitting in the fridge. It seemed that these days she lived in borrowed rooms with borrowed furniture, and sometimes she even felt that her life was just borrowing time in some other reality. But now, as she placed her hand on the folder, she felt like this moment was real.

She sat at the small dinette that rested under a tiny window that she could crack and smoke with little guilt of stinking up the whole place. Angie settled in with the folder and a pack of cigarettes, her lighter, and an empty coffee cup. She thought she should get up and put some water on, but she couldn't make herself move away from the folder.

She was fiercely independent. It took a major miracle for her to depend on anyone, but she had depended on Peter to find this information. In college, they were a great team. She would come up with ideas for papers and he would do the legwork. He was especially gifted at finding documents that were probably not meant to be found. He was part hacker, part bloodhound, and part psycho terrier with a taste for a pants leg. When he latched onto a goal, he did not let go until he was finished. He was thorough and, because of his OCD, his information was always cross-checked and verified.

She lit a cigarette and opened the folder. Peter had placed everything he found in backward chronological order. She noted the colored binder clips - his version of coding - and was not surprised since she knew his obsessive-compulsive habits. *God, I love this man*, she thought as she began her own investigation into her mother's past.

The death certificate confirmed what she already knew. Her mother was institutionalized. Veiled hints from foster family members had clued her in long ago. Angie reread the death certificate to make sure she didn't miss any details. Her eyes also focused on the birth date, October 2nd, 1945. *My mother's birthday.* Her breath caught in her throat as images of birthdays that they had both missed flashed through her mind. The only thing that was odd was the listing of Annabelle's parents. They should have been on the document, but it was blank. She knew that Annabelle's parents had lived in Harmon Springs. Her foster family had told her that much. Angie paper clipped it to help her remember to explore more later and moved to the next document.

The medical records. For a moment, she wondered how Peter was able to find them. He was tenacious; she was aware of that. She also knew that it was notoriously difficult to find medical records of patients in mental hospitals. The records were tabbed together with a bright blue binder clip. Annabelle was physically healthy, experienced early menopause, was diagnosed with melancholy, and had given birth to two children. Angie reread that last fact. *Two children.* Her field of vision began to narrow into a tight black tunnel. There were two? The pinpoint of light disappeared.

At the table, the cigarette burned itself out in the empty ashtray. The night birds sang their goodnight songs filling the late spring night with a sleepy tune. The sound of children at play far away floated on the evening air. At the table, a young woman lay face down, eyes partly open, seeing nothing, and unknowingly, seeing everything.

Chapter Two
Harmon Springs, Ga
1963

Angels can fly, I saw one once.
It flew the other way
And left me alone
With my questions
and my heart
That beats
only for her.

"Annabelle. It's time to go." The uniformed man stood at the front door, unsmiling. He was the local sheriff in the small southern town of Harmon Springs. Though it was the early 1960s, it could have easily a century earlier. The town prided itself in the strict preservation of an older way of life.

The town square consisted of a historical construction of a gothic court house, and was filled with antique stores, an old-world pharmacy, a bank, and a post office where loyal citizens picked up their mail. Plenty of locally-owned mom and pop diners, curiosity shops, a couple bookshops, and ancient pubs lined the nooks and crannies of the cobblestone and brick streets.

The one elementary school that stood at the north end of the town loyally taught the local youth up through the eighth grade; the high school that stood on the south end of the town graduated hard-working citizens. The schools acted as sentinels for education and reflected the town's pride in its children.

On the far edge of this old-world town, Annabelle stood, wringing her hands and looking at her baby, sound asleep in the bassinet. In her mind, she knew he was right. *I've done a bad thing. I don't remember doing it, but I know it's my fault.* She knew she was afraid of her son. She knew that there were times when whole hours would go by and she could not recall what happened. *Angel would be better off without me. I'm a failure as a mother. She deserves better. But how can I let her go? Angel is all I have left.*

Sheriff Clyde Harrison stepped further into the small, dirty, dry-rotting house, letting Martha Simpson in. The Simpson's had agreed, after much-heated persuasion, to take in the baby girl. Annabelle watched the woman go to the bassinet and pick up her Angel. Annabelle moved towards Martha, but Clyde was faster as he stepped in between them.

"Now, Annabelle, you know you can't take care of her on your own." He held Annabelle back with his hands firmly on her shoulders. "She'll have a good Christian home, and you're goin' to go to the hospital to get some help. Remember what we agreed on?" He continued holding her so that she would not stop Martha Simpson. She peeked around him and saw the woman walk out of the front door with her Angel.

"But, I didn't get to say goodbye...but I... didn't get to say..." she wailed as the Sheriff pulled her along and put her in his patrol car.

Clyde Harrison would never forget that day. The cry of grief and pain haunted him for the rest of his life. Her agony echoed, like an animal, a dying animal. He needed to get her to the doctor so that he and Ken could sign off on the paperwork to have her committed to Iron Rope.

He started his cruiser, glanced in the rearview mirror, alerted by the silence. Annabelle was mute, looking forward at nothing. He wasn't sure what was worse, the howl of pain or the profound, haunting silence. He put the car in gear and drove away and dust flew up, a parting curtain.

Later, Annabelle sat shivering on the examining table. The metal surface was cold through her thin clothes. She couldn't remember the last time she had bathed. The babies kept her busy. The doctor was asking her questions. He had kind eyes, and he was so young. He didn't seem like a doctor.

She was trying to remember what happened to Jacob. She desperately wanted to answer the doctor who was holding her hands in his. But that day was so hazy in her memory.

They had lain down for a nap. She was so tired. When she woke up, her mother was there going through their laundry. Her mother was angry at her, but she couldn't remember why. The voices were whispering in her ear. They wanted to tell her something, but she was hitting her head on the wall so they would go away. She thought she told her mother that something was wrong with Jacob. Then her mother was on the phone, calling her father. Something happened.

Something bad. Her mother was backing away from her. *Was she afraid of me?* What happened? Her mother was crying, holding her Angel. *Where was Jacob?* She couldn't remember where he was. She could see her mother's mouth moving, but she could not hear her over the shrill voices in her head.

Later the sheriff told her that she killed her baby. She remembered her mother crying and repeating *why, why, why.* Annabelle could not remember killing Jacob, so she did not know how to answer "why." The voices warned her not to speak because *they* might take Angel. She was too afraid even to ask who "they" were.

Now a doctor was asking her if she had killed her baby. She wanted to answer him but the voices warned her. They told her that if she talked to him, "they" would kill Angel too. She was afraid. She saw her father walk by the room. He could save her. She remembered running after him. She fell at his feet. She needed him to save her and to protect her Angel. She remembered him kicking her away. She knew at that moment that all hope was lost. She was lost. Annabelle sat, cold, alone, and mute to the kind doctor's questions and reassurances.

When the sheriff escorted her to the car, for that final ride, she did not fight. She made a vow not to speak. *No one cares.* The voices whispered, *no one cares...no one cares...*

Chapter Three
Iron Rope Sanatorium
1970

Therapy Session 237.
Patient: Annabelle Mason.
Diagnosis: Hysteria/Melancholy.

"Okay, Annabelle, let's talk about you," the young doctor looked down at his chart out of habit, but he knew it by heart "Hmm, okay, children. Tell me about them."

Annabelle looked outside, tired of the questions. *Over and over again, the same questions.*

"Tell me first about Angela. What kind of baby was she?" He tapped his pen on the chart.

"Her name is Angel," she whispered.

"Right, Angel." He wrote something on her chart.

She wondered, vaguely, what he wrote. *How could there possibly be anything new to write?* She whispered her same answer. "Angel is my sweet baby. Her daddy was a ghost, a spirit. He came to me and told me that I would have a beautiful Angel. But when I gave birth, the midwife said that Angel wouldn't be an appropriate name, so I named her Angela." It all came out in one breathy hum, a stock answer for a stock question.

He was writing more notes. She sat.

"Mmmm, okay, so you had two children, correct?"

"No."

"Annabelle, I know you delivered twins. What happened to your son?" His tone sounded weary to her, almost as if he was as tired of asking as she was of hearing the questions.

She sighed and was about to speak but the whispering began. It caught her off guard, though by now, she knew that it should not. She jumped in her seat and tried to speak, but as she opened her mouth, the whispers escalated to shrieks in her ears. Screeching, high-pitched banshee sounds pummeled her body. She screamed, but she was sure that no one could hear her over the chaos of shrieking. She covered her ears and banged her head on the table. The doctor calmly, reservedly, with a little bit of hesitation, pushed a button and orderlies entered instantly, injected her and carried her back to her room. The doctor made a final note in Annabelle's chart.

"Patient is delusional and uncooperative. Patient is highly recommended for lobotomy and solitary confinement."

Hours later, Annabelle opened her eyes to her dim gray room. Her cot was soiled. No voices. The last voice whispered to her that the doctor was going to erase her memories and that there would be no more pain. Her hand moved instinctively to her abdomen, saddened at the thought of losing Angel forever, but relieved at forgetting the other. She turned carefully onto her back. She was sore. She felt along her body. The sore parts told her that he had taken advantage of her again. There was no one to tell. She rolled over her to her side. It helped when she cried; the tears and mucus could roll out on its own. She grasped desperately onto all of her memories of her sweet baby. She didn't want to lose her Angel. She remembered her soft baby smell. She remembered her sweet smiles and coos. But there was that shadow of something evil, heavy, and dead that crouched in the corner of her mind. He would not let her forget.

Chapter Four
Harmon Springs
1963 - January

"Annabelle, push! It's time, push now!" The midwife was not pleased with this job. Annabelle was young, unmarried, and (everyone in the town knew it) crazy. The town had quietly watched the whole story unfold throughout these later months. Some said that it was probably a local man, drunk one night, and thought that crazy Annabelle would be easy pickings. Some said it was probably someone just passing through - a man who happened upon her during one of her bizarre midnight walks through the town and the fields. Most folks liked the idea of it being a stranger. The local wives did not like the idea of their husbands or sons lying with the crazy girl, even if they were drunk.

The midwife checked the dilation. She could see that it was time. "Push girl, push!"

Annabelle was gasping for air, trying to push, trying to muster the strength.

"I see the head!"

Annabelle pushed and out came a beautiful baby girl, and even under the birth muck, the midwife recognized the perfect features of the new baby girl. The midwife quickly cut the cord, wiped her off, bundled her up, and placed her on Annabelle's chest.

"I think I'll name her Angel."

The midwife turned to clean up the towels and mess. "Well now, I don't think that name would be appropriate. What about somethin' similar," her suggestion trailed off into nowhere.

Annabelle felt the sting of her words, but the sting could not outweigh the pure joy that she held in her arms. "Angela then. My sweet Angel." Another contraction. She screamed this time. Loudly.

"It's okay girl; it's just the afterbirth." The midwife shook her head in aggravation as she grabbed the pan to catch it in, but what she caught was not afterbirth. It was another baby. A boy. A strange boy. A silent, but wide awake boy. A boy that was thin and dry. His head was oddly swollen and he had large, knowing eyes. "Oh, Annabelle. You have twins." As she held him, she sensed there was something that didn't feel right. He was too heavy. Too dense. Too aware.

The midwife whispered a prayer and crossed her chest. She cut his cord, cleaned him up, and placed him next to the first baby. He immediately, with action faster and with more accuracy than a newborn should have, reached over and covered Angela's nose and mouth with his thin, barely formed hands.

"Oh no, little one." The midwife re-tucked his arm into his blanket.

Annabelle stared at the second baby. The midwife could not hear the voices. *The boy is evil...he is an abomination...beware...danger...* they whispered in Annabelle's ears. Annabelle knew that this child was not supposed to be, and that he shouldn't be. She didn't like to listen to the voices, but something told her that this time, they were right. She looked up helplessly at the midwife who was busily packing up her things, blatantly avoiding eye contact.

"Now you keep to bed. Your mother will be here shortly, but you all just rest. I have to go. Another birth is due tonight." She turned to face the girl on the bed. "Good luck, and may God be with you child." She turned and could not move out of that place fast enough.

Annabelle wondered who she was blessing as she watched the midwife left them alone.

Two months later, Sheriff Clyde Harrison knocked quietly at the mayor's slightly open door to the city hall meeting chamber. He noticed that Ken Mason, the mayor, and his best friend, was looking out the window and taking a drink of something in a one-shot movement. The sheriff cleared his throat, knowing his purpose for this visit was difficult and necessary. Clyde watched the mayor turn and sit at his desk. Ken focused on the spot just beyond the sheriff's left ear. Clyde knew that Ken was never sober; it was an unspoken vice between them.

"Hello Clyde, what can I do for you?" Continuing to avoid eye contact, the mayor closed folders acting like he was busy doing something. Clyde had a fleeting memory of something his wife said about Ken, that he was a handsome, well-bred man who knew no limits. She had no idea how right she was.

"Ken, you know why I'm here."

"You don't need to lecture me. I'm not in the mood."

"Ken, you have to do somethin'. You know she's too feeble-minded to take care of them babies. You need to…"

"No. I mean, yes, I know." Annabelle's father dropped his head into his hands after interrupting Clyde. Clyde wondered how this powerful man could run a whole town but not have one ounce of control over his daughter. Without looking up, Ken replied, "I will send her mother to stay with her." He lifted his head and avoided the concerned eyes of his good friend. "She'll help Annabelle until we can figure something out."

Clyde thumped his hat and left the room without speaking. He didn't know what to say. His uneasy feeling lingered like the remnants of a bad dream that stays all day long.

1963 June

Clarisse riffled through the mounds of clothes piled on the bed. It was one of many piles of clothes, diapers, and trash that were covering every floor in the house. "Anna, you have to keep things better. You will get you and the babies sick livin' like this. You can't stay healthy with all this filth around." She threw a soiled, moldy cloth diaper in a pile for trash. *Where did it all go wrong? She told him that Annabelle wasn't ready for this. They should never have let her move out.* Clarisse shook her head.

"I know, mom. I'm just so tired." Annabelle sat on the floor in the corner of the room, picking the peeling paint from the boards that made up the wall.

"Well, tired or not, you have other people to think about, not just yourself. You need to get it together –" Clarisse noted her daughter's limp dishwater colored hair. Under the filth, she knew there was a beautiful girl with perfect porcelain skin, perfect upturned nose, and perfect heart-shaped lips.

"Mom." Annabelle dropped her head and whispered, "I don't know about him." Annabelle's statement was void of emotion. She gestured listlessly towards the bassinets.

Clarisse looked over towards the baby beds. "Girl, what do you mean 'him'? You mean Jacob, your baby boy? What *is* your problem?" Clarisse threw another moldy, dirty diaper into the trash pile with more force than she had intended.

"Momma, there's something wrong with him. He don't eat. He don't cry." Annabelle covered her mouth as if she had said too much.

Clarisse threw down the clothes she was sifting through and walked over to the bassinets. In the one, Angela was sleeping soundly. She looked over to the other bassinet. There was no baby. She turned to face her daughter. Annabelle was now rocking, hitting the back of her head on the wall. Clarisse walked over to Annabelle, guided her up by her shoulders. She could smell unwashed skin, unwashed girl. Trying to breathe through her mouth only, she forced Annabelle's face to look at hers. "Annabelle, where is Jacob. Where is he?"

Annabelle, face devoid of any emotion, whispered, "He is in his bed, mom. There is something wrong with him."

Clarisse shook her head in confusion. She backed away from her daughter. "Sweetie, where is he?"

"There's something wrong with him, momma."

Clarisse backed towards the phone attached to the wall. She picked up the receiver, never taking her eyes off her daughter. She watched Annabelle slink down the wall and continue to bang her head. "It's okay, sweetie. I'm just going to call dad. We will figure this out." She dialed the rotary phone, unsure of how to explain this to her husband.

Ken Mason picked up the phone with his customary greeting, "Mason residence." He sounded tired; Clarisse knew in just those few syllables that he had already started drinking.

"Ken, honey, it's me."

"What's wrong?"

"Jacob's not in his bassinet. I don't know where he is, and neither does Annabelle."

The line was silent. "Ken, are you still there? Ken..."

"Yes, are you sure?"

"Am I sure what? That he's gone? Or that I'm inconveniencing you? God Ken, the baby is missing. I think that Annabelle –"

"Just keep it together. I'll call Clyde and be out there in a minute."

She heard the phone hang up on his end. She replaced the receiver with deliberate action. She needed to get the other baby away from Annabelle. Annabelle was now sitting still, stony-faced, staring into a void of nothing. Angela whimpered in her baby dreams as she awakened. Clarisse automatically went to her and checked her diaper. On autopilot, she changed it and held the baby close.

Clarisse did the grandma bounce and kept an eye on Annabelle. "It's okay sweetie, what a good girl you are," she cooed. Clarisse bounced and walked backward, trying to get out the front door without disturbing Annabelle's trance. She had never known Annabelle to be dangerous during her "episodes," but now Jacob was missing. Now she had doubts.

Clarisse whispered, "Annabelle, I'm going to step outside with Angela. We are just gonna get some fresh air." She reached back to open the front door, not turning away from the disheveled mess that she hardly recognized as her daughter. Annabelle didn't move. Clarisse took Angela outside into the warm evening air.

Chapter Five
Chicago
2000

He clutches the bottle,
And she knows it is too late -
He is gone into a sublime
Made up world
Of lust and desire that didn't involve her.
Eyes turned up, breathing labored,
She handed him the keys.

Angie woke to a quiet apartment. She checked her watch, midnight. Four hours. She shook the fog from her brain. She whispered to the empty room, "I had a brother." She stood, trying to un-cramp her body. Angie moved with wooden steps to the fridge for some water. Two children. She gulped water from a reused milk jug. Maybe this is more than I can handle on my own. She placed the jug back in the fridge. Standing, facing the refrigerator, she was at a loss. Should she call Peter? Should she handle this on her own? She grabbed her phone from her purse and sat back at the small table. Was this the news he thought would be too hard for her to handle?

She sat with her phone in her hand and marveled at the thought of a brother. How many days and nights did she sit alone in her room wishing she had a brother or sister? She remembered coveting friends who had siblings, hanging around their homes, trying to incorporate herself into being a part of their families. One friend once asked, half-joking, half not, if Angie wasn't friends with her just because she wanted to hang out with her older sisters. Angie remembered laughing it off as pure silliness.

But she did love pretending to be a part of a large, loving family. She loved watching sisters and brothers fighting, playing, sharing secrets, wanting to feel like an accepted part of a family. This was her one weakness, this longing; well, that, and smoking. Smoking was the one nasty habit she wished she never picked up. She loved it. She hated it.

She sat back down looking at the stack of papers. Without looking at the pack, she took out a cigarette and lit it. All this time I had a brother? She inhaled deeply and tried to pinpoint her feelings. Surprised? Very much so. Happy, yes. Angry, yes. Her foster parents had to have known about her brother. They never said a word. There were no hints at all. This had to be a mistake. She had little faith in her fellow human beings; in their ability for follow-through and truthfulness, but she just couldn't believe they would never tell her. Either Peter messed up, or she misread, and she was sure she hadn't misread.

She put the phone on the desk and marveled at the pile of papers. Peeking out from the collection was a copy of a faded newspaper article. She pulled it out. It was from her mom's hometown of Harmon Springs.

> July 2, 1963
> Baby Still Missing
> The baby of Miss Annabelle Mason, Jacob Mason, has been missing now for five days. Town volunteers have searched within a 40-mile radius for the missing child. He was last seen sleeping in his cradle. Miss Annabelle Mason, daughter of Mayor and Mrs. Mason, has been questioned and placed at the Iron Rope Sanatorium. If you see or know anything about Jacob Mason, please call Sheriff Clyde Harrison.

Underneath the article was a faded picture of twin babies. Angie noticed that one baby was healthy-looking and smiling, though the photo was blurry. She noticed the other baby was unsmiling and sickly looking; too thin for a healthy baby. It was her and her brother. A brother. I had a brother. His name was Jacob. What happened to him? She brought the picture closer to better see the thin baby. Dread climbed up her spine with its sharp claws. Whatever happened to him was not good. She slid the article aside and continued reading through the documents.

Chapter Six
Harmon Springs
1963 June

I hold onto dreams
That shatter.
When he walks
Through my door
He has the power,
All the power.

Annabelle sat in her yard with her babies. The summer morning held the hint of a cool breeze left over from lazy spring days. She closed her eyes and faced the sun, absorbing the rays gratefully. Angel playfully kicked in the air, smiling and giggling at her mother. Jacob lay still, his head slightly turned towards his sister. He did not blink enough. Annabelle was sure of this. He was wasting away. He held no food, no water, no milk. He was all skull and baby bird-like bones. She changed his diaper only because she felt she should, but not because it was necessary. He didn't eliminate anything. She knew this wasn't right. She didn't like the way he stared at Angel. She reached for Angel protectively and held her up to the sun. Angel squealed in delight. Jacob slowly followed them with his eyes, watching.

Annabelle stood and gathered Angel's blankets to place her in the bulky double stroller. She kissed Angel's head as she laid her down. Annabelle reached uncertainly for Jacob. Lifting him filled her with instant anxiety. He was both weightless and heavy. There was that moment of alarm whenever she lifted him. He should weigh next to nothing, but he was oddly heavy, like somehow he was hiding four twenty-five pound weights in his pajamas. She wrapped his arms tightly to his sides using the receiving blanket, and then placed him alongside Angel for the short ride back into the house.

Feeding and naptime were dreaded times for Annabelle. Angel was no problem; she ate all that was given to her. She slept when she was supposed to. Jacob, though, was more challenging. He refused all food. He refused to sleep. She fed Angel and put her down for her nap. She didn't attempt to feed Jacob and laid him down in his bassinet. He could not see Angel; however, his head was facing her bassinette, as though he could. Annabelle took a half step back, unsure of what to do. She was so tired. She stood, watched him watching her Angel.

A breeze shuttered through the house. She heard the faint stirrings of the whispers. Quietly in her ear, they chanted, "he is planning, he is planning, he is planning..." Annabelle turned and covered her Angel, who was already sleeping peacefully. She half walked, half stumbled to a small spot that was clear on her bed. She fell deeply asleep between piles of dirty laundry, mixed with clean.

Chapter Seven
Chicago
2000

The night nurse comes in,
Concern on her face,
Weathered deep into her skin –
Years of sadness and pain –
I hear my voice crack
To tell her
How much I love you.

"Yes, I know...okay...yes...I will." Angie finished the call with Peter. She knew he meant well, but she also knew this was a job for her, alone. She wasn't sure what Harmon Springs was like now, but she had a sneaky suspicion that they would not be super excited to see an obviously gay man flaunting down its pristine, non-diverse, historic streets. Besides, she operated alone, that was the best way. If anything was screwed up, it would only be her fault. Her purpose was clear. She was going to retrace her mother's last steps, starting at the sanatorium, and then backtrack to Harmon Springs, following her mother's first steps.

She took one more look around her apartment. The files were tucked safely away in her bag, her cigarettes safe in her purse, and her few articles of clothing were folded neatly in an overnight bag. She wondered fleetingly what the downstairs neighbor would complain about since she was going away for a couple of days. It was early in the morning; the sun was just up.

As she turned onto the last landing, she came face to face with him. "Good morning Mr. Willis. How are you today?"

"Well, maybe now I can get some sleep since you are leaving," he sneered and nodded to her overnight back. He put his hands on his bony hips and stepped out of her way.

"I hope so, sir." She didn't have time to fight with him. She shoved her way past.

He called after her, "I hope you don't come back. I would rather live with the ghosts."

She pretended not to hear and left the building.

Hours later, she was driving 85 mph down a long country highway. She would find out what happened to her twin brother, and her mother. There was nothing in the paperwork, other than the newspaper report about Jacob. She assumed the baby was never found. She smoked her seventh cigarette of the day with purpose. Why was it, when a woman freaked out, the first answer was to institutionalize her? Why was it that women had no choice in the matter, as if they were less than human? She shook her head and snubbed out her cigarette. I really need to stop smoking in my car.

The solemn setting sun let her know that she had not eaten since early morning. From her map, she could see that she was still over eight hours away from Iron Rope. She pulled off at the next exit that promised food, gas, and lodging. The idea of covered and smothered fried chicken made her insides rumble. She spied the tried and true restaurant, the Cracker Barrel, and noted the Holiday Inn snuggled up next to it. Her job sent her all over the country opening restaurants and consulting for failing restaurants. This was one chain that she never worked with; and she liked to keep it that way. Knowing the inner workings of eating establishments tended to influence her appetite, usually for the worse.

She pulled into the parking lot, turned off the car, and called Peter.

"Hi Angie. What's up? Are you stopping for the night?"

"Yes, I'm going to get a quick bite to eat, stay at the Holiday Inn here, sleep a couple hours and then leave early and arrive at Iron Rope by lunch tomorrow. I need you do me a favor."

"Of course, that's what I'm here for. I really feel like I should be there with you."

"Thanks Peter, but I just need some consistent cell service. I'm not sure they even know that there are such things as cell towers down here."

"Okay, what do you need me to look up?"

She could hear the amusement in his voice and she felt comforted.

"Can you get me the number of the director again? I seemed to have misplaced it. I need to call him and confirm our meeting."

Peter laughed into the phone, "I'll call you back and put it in your voice mail. Angie, be safe."

"I will. Thanks, friend. I've got to go get some food and rest."

"What? You mean you can't live on cigarettes and pure determination?"

"Ha. I wish. Call ya later."

"Okay, bye!" He hung up. It was always startling how he said good-bye on the phone, so suddenly. She gathered her purse, threw her phone into it, and stepped out of her car. Her legs screamed, but it was a good scream.

Luckily, it was an off time for the restaurant so she was seated right away. She placed her order and continued her research on Iron Rope. Peter had dug up plenty of reading material.

Iron Rope was a catchall mental institution for three counties. It had been a stop for the Underground Railroad, which was interesting. How old was this place? She didn't know much about mental asylums, not much more than what mainstream horror flicks showcased. She knew that the oldest one was up in Maine or Vermont. She recalled that from some high school research paper...did she ever finish that paper? She cocked her head. Underground Railroad. What year was that, like 1840? I have to remember to ask Peter about that.

She flipped through some more documents and stopped at a 1920s snapshot of the building and grounds. It looked like the traditional four story building complete with ghosts and sordid histories. It was huge and stood with an air of superiority.

The server placed the covered and smothered chicken down in front of Angie. "Whatcha got there sweetie?"

Angie was startled. "Oh, um, it's the Iron Rope Mental Institution…uh…sanatorium; in the 20s, I think." Angie shut the folder.

"Oh! I've heard of that place! I heard it is like all haunted and stuff. Didn't it close down in the 80s?"

"Well, I hope not, since I'm supposed to be there for an appointment tomorrow," Angie laughed a bit too loud. She felt instantly self-conscious as the older couples looked her way accusingly. Note to self, do not upset the old people. Geeze.

The server eyed her trying to see if she was joking or not. "I'm pretty sure it was closed down, I saw it on the news and stuff. Well, anyways, I bet it will be good ghost hunting for ya! I heard that ghost hunting show was going to feature it this fall and stuff…I can't wait."

Angie stared at the server, trying to see if she was joking. They both blinked at each other for three heartbeats.

"Well, okay, if you need anything let me know and stuff." The server smiled, an unsure smile, and turned and walked away.

"Thanks, *and stuff*." Angie added under her breath as she shuffled her gravy and hash browns around her chicken. Closed? The server had to be confusing Iron Rope with some other sanatorium. She had just spoken with the director last week. He was more than accommodating about her mother's history and seemed pleased to be able to help. His secretary helped her make an appointment with him. Angie took some halfhearted, dainty, tasteless bites.

She sipped her sweet tea, a delicacy in the South she well knew, and figured that Iron Rope still existed, but probably in a newer facility. Her phone vibrated on the table. One of those older couples looked disapprovingly at her. She smiled her sweetest "bite me" smile and answered.

"Hey, I was going to leave you the number, you weren't supposed to answer."

"I know, but I just spoke with a server and she says that Iron Rope closed down in the 80s "and stuff." Do you think you could double check things?"

"Sure, but didn't you just talk to them? What's and stuff?"

"Just a weird thing the server kept saying. And yes. I did just talk to them. Maybe the server is confused. Give me the number again."

"Yup. She sounds reliable and stuff," he laughed into the phone. It was good to hear him laugh.

She scribbled the number on a napkin and hung up, eyeing the older couple who kept stealing angry glances at her.

She finished her food, paid the bill, and walked over to the hotel. If she was on the road by 3 a.m., she should be at Iron Rope by noon - that should give her plenty of time.

Her exit was coming up. The directions were clear. Take Exit 12, turn right, and go for 34 miles. Iron Rope Sanatorium will be on the left. Exit 12 popped up, unassuming. No traveler stops, or gas signs.

She turned and then turned right. Thirty-four miles and then she might have some answers. The two-lane road was quiet and dotted with distant farms and crops of something she could not identify. It was odd that she did not pass one car, not one truck, not one slow moving farm vehicle.

She saw the building looming in the distance. It looked out of place, so large, and unnatural, like some great god of architecture plunked it down in a haphazard decision because he didn't know what to do with it. Nature was reclaiming it, and it was obvious even from a distance. As she drove nearer, her heart dropped and a warning buzzing filled her ears. It was obviously deserted. She parked her car and stepped out into the warm air, phone in hand. The building had been abandoned for a long time. No windows remained…the outside walls were covered with ivy, mold, and cracks. The graffiti, though now faded, showed that there were young people in the area at one time. She leaned on her car and hit speed dial.

"Hey Angie, shouldn't you be meeting…"

"Peter. It *is* abandoned. There's nothing here but a rotting old sanatorium." Why does nothing work out for me?

"That's impossible! There are no other listings. Did you talk to the director this morning?"

"Yes, I spoke with his secretary and she confirmed my appointment. She said that he was looking forward to meeting me."

"Call him back. I must have made a mistake somewhere Angie. Sorry."

This is exactly why I like working alone. You trust someone to do one thing, and it gets screwed up, 9 times out of 10. She reigned in her frustration, "It's okay, I'll call him. I'll call you back in a few."

"Okay, sorry Angie."

This time she hung up on him abruptly. She dialed the director's number.

"Iron Rope Sanatorium, this is Karen, how can I help you?"

"Umm, hello Karen, this is Angie Simpson, I have a meeting today with Doctor Austin."

"Oh, yes, hello Miss Simpson! Didn't we speak earlier?"

"Yes, yes we did. So, I am kind of embarrassed because I am standing out front of an abandoned building and I think I might have my directions mixed up."

"Oh, I see! Well, are you at 143 Route 2?"

"Yes."

"And, are you looking at a seemingly deserted large structure that is a little worse for wear?"

Angie looked at the building that was casting a large shadow over her in the afternoon sun, "Yes, ma'am, that is what I see," though she thought "a little worse for wear" was too kind of a description.

"Well, that's it! People sometimes think we are abandoned; we haven't had a lot of funding these days. The newer part of the building is behind the old building. Shall I send someone out front to meet you?"

"Yes, that would be nice."

"Okay, someone will be with you shortly."

Angie shoved her phone unceremoniously in her purse. She thought for a moment that she should try to call Peter and tell him that she was at the right place. She grabbed her phone back from her purse and saw that it had no signal. "Great." She slammed it back in her purse.

She checked the road again; there were no other cars in sight. She turned to take a better look at the building now standing in shadow. The boarded windows glowered in the shade. Where the main doors should be, old weathered boards were nailed in an attempt to seal it up. Even from this distance, she could see that no one had used those front doors for years. She mumbled to herself, "What is going on here? Maybe I need to visit a real nut house." She turned to open her car door, not defeated, but confused and disappointed - in herself, in Peter, in her foster parents, even in Dr. Austin and his too nice nurse.

While fumbling for her keys, she heard the echo of footsteps. She walked cautiously up to the boarded doors; the footsteps seemed to echo from behind the door. Someone was coming.

The boarded door opened without a sound and a nurse walked out of the shadows. It was alarming to see it move since on first inspection, it looked like it hadn't moved in years.

"Hello? Ma'am?" Angie wanted to make sure that the nurse could see her.

"Yes, hello Miss Simpson? Sorry about the mess." The nurse pushed aside the boards like they were a swinging door and gestured Angie to come inside.

Angie put a hesitant foot forward.

"Sorry about the dark hallway. There is no electricity in this part of the building." The nurse smiled reassuringly, guiding Angie down the long corridor. "Doctor Austin is expecting you. Right this way."

Angie was finding it difficult to keep up with the brisk walking nurse. Slightly out of breath, she asked, "So, is this part of the building not used?" What a dumb question, she regretted asking it immediately.

The nurse laughed quietly. "Oh, this part is of no use to us. Funds are very low these days; we spend any money that the state gives us on our patients. Right this way miss."

Chapter Eight
Harmon Springs
2000

He touches the fabric,
Stiff and ancient,
But the boy is long gone
His body was just a vessel,
Given in love
And joy
To his hero and savior.

"Can I help you young man?" The secretary noticed the stranger as soon as he walked through the door of the Harmon Springs Sheriff's Office. He was young, good looking, but there was something oddly feminine about him.

Peter walked up to the counter. "Yes ma'am. My name is Peter Chancellor." He held out his hand over the counter to her.

She shook his hand slowly, "Nice to meet you Mr. Chancellor. How can I help you?"

Peter smiled reassuringly at the forty-odd year-old woman. He couldn't help but note her smock that was too large for her ample frame and her flip flops were rejects from a trash heap somewhere. He made sure his face didn't register the fashion faux paus. "I am looking for a friend of mine. She would have been here about three days ago? Her name is -"

"Sir, I am sorry, but you're the first stranger I've seen in about six months. People just don't usually come through here. I'm sorry I can't help ya." She smiled sweetly and resumed her filing duties. As she turned around, he was assaulted with evidence of a bad home perm and dye job.

Peter didn't move. "Ma'am? I'm sorry to bother you, but can I leave her picture or fill out a missing person's report?"

The secretary turned back to him and smiled condescendingly. "Well, now, I would love to help you young man, but the sheriff is not in and I just don't think we could do a missing person's report since she's not really a resident of our town."

"Since when do you have to be a resident?"

"Sir, I am going to ask you to leave. She isn't here, she never was here." Her smile was gone.

Peter rolled his eyes. "Okay, well then can you give me directions to Iron Rope Sanatorium?" He knew his directions had to be correct, but when he was supposed to come across the exit, he missed it in his bleary-eyed state. He had been on the road since he had lost contact with Angie. Traveling this last twelve grueling hours, grinding away the miles into the Deep South, filled him with anxiety. The farthest south he had been was the South Suburbs in Chicago. This was not anywhere he wanted to be. All he knew about the South was from the movies and none of the movies were particularly gay friendly. Once he realized he missed the exit, he saw the exit that brought him to Harmon Springs. Maybe Angie had missed the exit too and was looking at some other abandoned large building.

The smile still gone, the woman cocked her head in a fake guise of sympathy, "Sir, that place has been closed down for years. If you are looking for mental help maybe you should try Savannah or some other large city." She turned, effectively dismissing him.

Wow, really? He turned, dismayed, and walked out of the office and ran into a large man with a badge. Oh, I do love a man in uniform.

"Excuse me, could you help me?" Now he could work his charm. He tossed his lock of naturally black hair that tended to hang distractedly over his eyes.

The sheriff, tall, trim, and ruggedly handsome, eyed him suspiciously. "Well now, what seems to be the problem?"

"I'm looking for a friend of mine and I think she may have come through here." He flashed his winning 'I'm a good guy smile.'

The sheriff scratched his head, "I don't think I've seen any strangers lately. What's her name?"

Peter handed him Angie's picture, "Her name is Angie, or um, Angela Simpson. She was actually from here."

The sheriff glanced half-heartedly at the picture and handed it back. "Well, I don't know no Angela Simpson, but you say she was from here? I know all the families 'round here. She's very pretty. Is she a girlfriend or a relative?"

"She's my good friend. She was coming here to find out about her mother and her baby brother. Her mother's name was Annabelle Mason. Is the Mason family still here?"

The Sheriff smiled a mask of innocence. "No, I'm sorry. Maybe you got your information mixed up. I don't think we can help you. Have a good day."

Peter watched him walk into a back office. This is not working. Man, I'm losing my touch. He dug his cell phone out of his pocket, no service. Great. He had no leads. He decided to backtrack and find that exit.

Suddenly exhausted, the Sheriff sat heavily in his chair. He remembered what his father, the sheriff before him, said just before he died. "Son, the past will always come back to haunt you. You do right the first time around." He knew Angie Simpson. He knew the story very well. His father warned him that Annabelle's daughter might come asking questions. The sins of the father had come to make their claim.

Sherriff Dale Harrison pulled out the map of the abandoned asylum, Iron Rope. He heard his father's words echoing in his memories, "Son, you will need to secure the funds to tear that place down. It ain't that you should, or ought to; it's that you have to." His father's wizened face concentrated into the coffee cup, cupped in his hands. In a whisper, he added, "I did what I could. I closed it down, but it always comes down to money."

"What, Dad?"

His father sat back and looked him straight in the eyes. "Son. You have to do it right the first time. The past will haunt you always. Now you're sheriff, so do it right."

"Okay, Dad."

He made the promise to his father, though at the time, he was unsure of what he was promising and what the cost would be. Neither man could know that the town would be hurt so badly economically. Kids graduated and moved away. The mill closed. The new highway bypassed them, leaving them long forgotten.

Times were tough. It was hard to convince the city
commissioners that money spent on demolishing the sanatorium was
money wisely spent. No one outside of Harmon Springs cared about
that place anymore. Iron Rope stood empty and abandoned. It was an
eyesore that no one looked at anymore. It was boarded up securely
and tucked away out of people's memories. There were more critical
needs on the books: the elementary school needed a new roof, the
courthouse basement still flooded after every rain, and the streets
were always needing repair.

Some more progressive town's folk were talking about adding
cell towers, wireless communications, and a super shop everything
in a one-stop store. As the young Sherriff refolded the plans, he
chuckled, thinking of his father rolling over in his grave. Old Clyde
would stand his ground against any of those newfangled ways of life.

"Jessica, can you come in here?"

The secretary stood at his door. "Yes, Sheriff?"

"If you see that young man again, you call me right away on the
radio."

"Yes, I will. Is he dangerous?" She had that eager anticipation in
her eyes for some real drama.

"No, no, he is not; I just would like to know what he is up to."

She shrugged and went back to her filing.

The sun was dipping dangerously low, but Peter caught the exit
this time. The two-lane highway was growing darker by the minute.
He realized he was whistling a tune from *Deliverance* when he saw
the faint outline of the massive building that must be the sanatorium.
He pulled up next to her car. Angie was right; the building was
abandoned. He tried her car doors, but they were locked. He turned
to face the boarded up front doors of the long-dead structure. She
must have gone in. He checked his cell phone. Still no service.

"Angie! Angela Simpson!" His voice bounced through the vacant
windows and disappeared down what to him sounded like
abandoned hallways. The sun was giving way to the dark. He walked

up to the boarded door and tried to find a way in. It was sealed and rusted tight with impossibly large nails. Maybe this is where 'dead as a doornail' came from, he thought as he stepped back to look up at the vast windows. "Angie!" He yelled again. "Okay," he spoke aloud, trying to convince himself, "I'm going to have to crawl through those horrible windows. Damn. I'm not wearing the right shoes for this." Then he heard the giggling. A small child giggling. He spun around, but there was no child.

"Angie?" he whispered. A clicking sound of footsteps on linoleum spun him around again. Was that someone coming? Coming from inside the abandoned asylum? "Angie? Is that you?" There was a creaking sound of old wood grinding along rusted nails. Peter stepped back again as the large boarded door opened. A nurse peered out at him.

"I am so sorry, Mr. Chancellor?"

Peter hesitated and muttered, "Yes?"

"Miss Simpson said you would be by; I just got caught up with my patients. Come this way, Mr. Chancellor, please pardon the mess. I'm so sorry for making you wait." She smiled and held the door open for him to enter.

In a barely audible whisper, he asked, "Is... Angie Simpson in there with you?"

"Why yes, please follow me, I will take you to her right away." She smiled and turned with confidence back down the long black, disintegrating hall.

Chapter Nine
Harmon Springs
1963 June

He looked down at her,
Staying still, so still.
Eyes full of disgust and rage
No pity, no love
He shook her loose forever,
His duty was more important.

Clyde Harrison stood still outside Annabelle's front door. He could hear rustling of blankets and her singing a soft lullaby. He waited for the song to end. He peered through the screen and watched Annabelle fall into her bed that looked like a mass of dirty clothes.

Somehow, he needed to make all of this right. Protecting his town and protecting his people was his job. It would be the job for his children and their children, and on through the ages. Now, he had to maintain the here and now. He didn't want to leave a dark legacy for his children. This was his mistake and Ken's mistake. It needed to be resolved. A fire would be believable, Ken was right. No one would be surprised by a house fire. It would probably even expected with this mess. His heart ached for those babies. He stood listening to Annabelle's snores. The gasoline was in his cruiser. If he did it right, they wouldn't suffer too much.

Wiping the sweat from his brow, he made his decision. Those babies should not suffer any more than they needed to. Lifting the latch of the screen door, he stepped into the house. The boards creaked with dry rot. Fat, well-fed roaches scattered. The acid rank of a prolonged roach infestation made his eyes water. He walked through the living room and into the one bedroom. The bassinets were to his left; Annabelle fast asleep was on his right.

He saw that the one baby, the odd one, was not asleep. His head was turned towards Angela's bassinet. He hadn't expected anyone to be awake. The Sherriff watched them all morning and figured they were worn out enough to be sleeping.

He picked up a ratty pillow that was topping a pile of trash and took a deep breath. This was mercy, he told himself. "Lord, give me strength." He held the pillow over the boy's face. The child didn't struggle or move. He had the strange sensation that the baby may have already been dead. His heart was pounding in his ears. He looked over at Annabelle; she was still snoring. He walked over to Angela's bassinet. God, what a beautiful baby. She was surrounded by a bright light that was streaming through the cracked window. She was smiling in some baby dream of happiness and hope.

He held the same pillow over her and Annabelle stopped snoring. He panicked. In a moment of confusion, he hesitated. He could not hurt that baby. She was innocent. This was crazy and he knew it. He glanced at the other baby. He never could figure out why he did it. What could have possessed him to do what he did next? He spent the rest of his years fixated on that moment.

He grabbed the baby boy's body and left the house. The body was oddly heavy for being obviously underweight. He put the baby's body in the trunk and put his cruiser in reverse without turning on the engine. No noise. He sat at the bottom of the hill and gripped his steering wheel, trying to ground himself.

The radio startled him. "Sheriff, there's a problem at Joe's, I think it's old man Abe, drunk and disorderly again." Static. "Sheriff?"

"Yes, I'm here. Send Deputy James. I'll be there directly."

"Okay, sir. And your mother called, she said that Mrs. Jessup's funeral will be tomorrow. She wanted to know if..."

"Okay, thank you, I'll call her back." He put his radio down and realized that he was sweating like it was the dog days of summer.

He sat in his cruiser rethinking the plan. Maybe he could solve the problem with minimum loss of life. If Annabelle was accused of Jacob's murder, the worse that would happen is time in a mental institution, especially since everyone knew she was 'not right.' He could find a home for Angela; he knew Ken could not raise her or really, should not. He whispered a prayer. Clyde Harrison had one thing to do before resuming regular duties. He made his way to the local funeral home.

"Well, hello, Sheriff! What can I do to help you today?" The mortician was a jovial man, much too jovial for the duties of his job.

"Hey, Herb. I was wondering if you had any of that amazing seasoning spice your wife makes. My Helen says we are out and I was in the area." Clyde casually flipped through the mortician's schedule that was open on the front desk.

Herb was caught off guard, "Well, I 'm sure she does. Can I have her bring it by later this evenin'? I'm kind of busy here today. Mrs. Jessup's funeral is scheduled for early tomorrow mornin', and I've got to get things in order, you know –"

"Oh, it's fine, I just thought I would stop by since I was passin' by. Mrs. Jessup was a fine lady. I remember she used to babysit my brothers and me. We sure were hard on her." The Sheriff smiled at the innocent childhood memories.

"Yes, sir, she was a fine lady. She died peacefully in her sleep. That's the best way to go, don't ya think?" The mortician winked at him.

"Well, yes, I'm in full agreement with that. I definitely would love to go that way. I also want a closed casket - that is for sure."

"I understand, but having it open gives the family closure. Of course, we would always comply with the deceased's wishes. I need to get Mrs. Jessup ready for her viewing and funeral tomorrow."

"I will have to remember to put the closed casket part in my will. I'll try to make it to her funeral. Thanks, and see you later."

"Sure thing Sheriff. I'll stop by later with the seasoning." The mortician slapped him good-naturedly on the back. From the angle they were standing, he could not see the moment of confusion in the Sheriff's eyes.

"Oh, yes! That will be great. I get off work at 8 p.m. or so." He tipped his hat and walked back to his cruiser with a plan in motion. It shouldn't be too difficult, later tonight, much later, he would deposit the baby into Mrs. Jessup's casket, conceal him in the folds of the many skirts he was sure she would be buried in.

Chapter Ten
Harmon Springs
1963 June

The mother cries
For the loss of her child
For the loss of her family
For the loss of her soul
She will miss the moments
That all parents take for granted
She will miss her baby
And die alone.

The warm evening settled around the man sitting alone on his porch. The smell of sweet honeysuckle and magnolia did not escape him, but he was not interested in the flora. It was time for a drink. He figured that his wife would still be working on finishing her quilting project. The coast would be clear to grab a drink from his hidden bottle of scotch.

He held the screen door so that it wouldn't slam and made his way to the wide-open kitchen. He was reaching for a glass when he heard footsteps behind him. He turned to see his wife, hands on her hips, accusing eyes that didn't need a voice to say what needed to be said. He casually turned and grabbed the glass and went to the sink. Her eyes were boring into his back. He filled the glass.

"No, Clarisse. We can't do anything to help her. Clyde is right; she needs to go to Iron Rope and get help. This is beyond our control. She killed her own baby. Our grandchild! What else can I do?" He gulped the sulfur-tinged water, unhappily. He avoided her puffy eyes.

Clarisse retaliated shakily to his back. "But you said you would handle this. She is our daughter. We have to stand by her. Maybe she didn't kill him. Can you not even give her some thought of kindness, some benefit of the doubt? What if he is out there somewhere? Please, Ken, we could –"

"No!" He turned to face her and slammed his glass on the thick wooden kitchen table. "We tried. We raised her the best we could. We've done our time." Clarisse sobbed, turned, and left the room.

Ken stood in the kitchen. He knew he was alone even when she was in the room. It wasn't only at home. He felt his town slowly losing faith in him as a leader. People avoided eye contact with him on the streets, and no one stopped by to talk politics or weather. He was used to being the fearless and respected leader of their perfect small town. He was handsome and loved by all. But now, now it was all slipping away.

Annabelle was supposed to be the savior of their relationship. Clarisse was heartbroken when the doctors said she could not have children. She loved children. All children. She had taught at the local elementary for 15 years. Every child felt loved in her presence.

When Clyde said he could help, Ken was overjoyed. Clyde warned him that he could not ask a bunch of questions. Annabelle came to them one night, swaddled tightly and perfect. That was the year of the drought, 1945.

"Clyde, she can't be more than a couple of hours old, where is she from?"

Clyde shuffled his feet. "All I can tell you is that the mother is a young teenager from another town, and she didn't want this baby. You have her free and clear."

"Okay, how do we explain her? People will notice we have a new baby. Everyone knows that Clarisse can't have children." He held the baby close, already falling in love with her.

"We'll just say you adopted her from a distant relative who was unable to care for her. They won't ask a lot of questions. Everyone loves Clarisse; they will all be pleased; she has her own child. Let's take her to Clarisse. It'll be fine, Ken. You're helping a young girl who made a mistake, and you are giving a new baby girl a perfect home. This is good."

It was good. Good for about three years. Then, there were signs. Imaginary friends, screaming fits that had no source, catatonic states, bizarre and hard to explain behavior. At three years of age, everyone in town knew that Annabelle, the beautiful child, was 'touched.' Clarisse had to take an extended sabbatical to home school Annabelle because her daughter, though beautiful, imaginative, and introspective, couldn't function in group settings.

Annabelle grew up alone. She had no friends. There were no sports games to take her to. There were no giggling sleep-overs with her friends. Just her. She sat in her room and drew odd pictures, and wrote bizarre poetry. As the years went by, Ken admitted to himself; she didn't even have an adequate father. He couldn't stand to be around her.

When Annabelle turned 18, they set her up a home on some property they had on the edge of town. Ken remembered how nervous Clarisse was, leaving Annabelle to fend for herself. Ken needed Annabelle out of the house, and he needed her out fast. It would only be a matter of time before she started showing.

He shook off his memories and took his empty glass to the pantry. The scotch bottle was behind the sack of flour. Standing in the pantry, he poured the drink and drank it quickly. He refilled the glass and re-hid the bottle and moved to sit on the empty front porch. Now one of the babies is gone, God knows where, though he had his suspicions. Annabelle is gone, and there is Angela. He could not face her. Every time he looked at her, he saw his own sin. There was a creak behind him.

"Ken, I know you think I'm too tired, or maybe too old, but I still think we could take a more active role in raising Angela. The Simpsons are fine folk, but we are her only family. Could you please rethink this?"

He didn't turn to face her. He knew she knew his drinking secret, though neither spoke of it aloud. But did she know his other secrets? He trusted only one other soul with his sins.

"She is already at the Simpson's. They have two other small children and they are young. She will blend right in just fine."

"How can you be so cold? My heart is breaking and you just sit here." She turned to go back inside the house, knowing he would not answer, and stopped short, "you know, I know Clyde arranged the Simpsons for Angela." Ken did not respond. "Yes, he is so good at finding homes for babies, isn't he? Just like you are good at finding a home for things you love." She left Ken sitting on the porch, dealing with his demons and drinking the only cure he knew.

Chapter Eleven
Iron Rope Sanatorium
2000

Peter was faced with two choices. Follow the crazy nurse or jump in his car and drive the hell away. "What the heck," he muttered, "I ain't afraid of no ghosts..." he smiled at his stupid sense of bravery and recollection of that campy movie and followed the now distant sound of the nurse's footsteps. He quickened his steps to catch up with her.

"Right this way, sir." Her voice echoed back to him. He caught a glimpse of her as she turned abruptly down a corridor.

He realized that he was now alone. Oh great, alone in an abandoned mental asylum. There is a crazy nurse who has disappeared, it's dark and I am pretty sure I am getting spider webs in my hair.

"Angie! Can you hear me?!" He walked tentatively forward; the hallway was dark, but the rooms with their door-less entries were even darker. He could hear water dripping somewhere, the wind blowing through the rooms, and something else. He cocked his head to hear better. Was that the sound of pages turning? "Angie! Are. You. Here?" The sound stopped. A door opened further down the hallway, spilling out light.

"Peter? Is that you?" The shadow stepped out of the room.

"Oh, my God! Girl, you about gave me a heart attack!" He ran to her. "What the hell is wrong with you? Why didn't you call me? I have been everywhere looking for you!" He stopped yelling as he stepped into the lighted room. It was a records room. The room was long, with aisles and aisles of boxes of records that he could not see the end of. His OCD kicked in and he itched to find the method of organization. Probably alphabetical, or maybe by year of death, or both. He shook his head and analyzed his good friend. She looked haggard, tired, but smiling.

Angie grabbed his hand and led him over to the desk where she was working. "This is what I've been doing." She shoved the large box that was labeled "Annabelle Mason" at him.

"Is this...all of her...belongings? How did you find this?" He looked at the pictures and random drawings spread all over the desk. He watched her sit, obviously exhausted. "How have you been staying alive? It's been three days! Where did you get this light?" He bent down to examine the rusty oil lamp. "Who was that nurse? What the hell is going on?"

Angie laughed as she sifted through the drawings. "Let me see if I can answer your questions in order, um, yes, this is all of my mom's belongings that she gathered during her time here." Angie stopped and looked at him and he felt like it was a truth check. He nodded to get her to keep talking. "She was here from 1963 until 1975. I've learned so much. I found this room because I too followed the nurse, but somehow, she got ahead of me. I was out of breath." He looked casually over at her full cigarette pack. "I stopped, and when I put my hand on the wall for support, the door to this room opened up. The lamps were in here already and I noticed there is enough oil for them to last another 100 years. Kind of weird, I know, like something from the movies..." she shrugged.

"Wait, you mean the crazy nurse left you and you just happened to 'find' this room, and there just 'happened' to be plenty of oil for light?" He picked up a drawing of a young female face.

"Yes, listen...there's so much more." Angie sat on a rusty chair and motioned for him to sit on the other chair. "The first day I spent looking for her things, I wasn't hungry or thirsty. Then the second day I woke up and I knew I was in trouble. I lost cell phone service right after my last call to you, so I knew that was not going to help me. I was so intent on finding her box; I hadn't noticed a shelf with a few snack staples. I had no idea how old they were, but I didn't care. Most of the boxes I opened had nothing edible in them. On a top shelf though, there was a trusty box of Twinkies. Everyone knows they last forever. Next to them was a jar of tomato juice. I sipped some of the tomato juice and ate a Twinkie and continued my search."

Peter recoiled at the thought of that particular combination. "Why didn't you just go back out to your car and get somewhere and call me?" He noticed that the Twinkies and tomato juice supplies had barely been touched as he could see the millennia ages of dust layered all over them. He also kept glancing at the full pack of cigarettes, unsure why the sight of them raised an uneasy feeling.

Angie looked up at him blankly.

"I don't know...I just didn't want to leave. I was afraid the room would disappear, like the nurse." She pushed a bound book into his hand.

"Wow, is this a diary?" he asked.

She smiled and nodded.

"Well, can you give me the *Reader's Digest* version?" He pushed it back to her.

"Yes, it's a crazy story." She rubbed the outside of the book as if it were something alive and thankful for her touch.

"Angie. Are you okay?" He watched her snap out of her reverie.

"Yeah, why?"

"You are just so out of it. You know we can gather this stuff up and take it to a hotel and get some, um, real food, and some real beverages and a shower might be nice for some of us..."

Angie smiled. "No, Peter, we can't really do that."

"What? The shower part? I didn't mean together..."

"No, the leaving part. We can't leave. We are dead."

Peter laughed and then stopped, caught up in the serious look on Angie's face. "Wait. What? There is no way I am dead. I can't be dead. I didn't even feel anything. I don't understand..."

"Peter, stop; you are whining. You died when you entered the sanatorium. Right at the front door, there is a caved in portion of the floor; that is why the front door was boarded over. You came to my light, Peter. This is my heaven and you are here with me." She smiled and twirled girlishly in her chair.

Peter touched his skin; it felt the same. "If I'm dead, then why can I still feel? Why am I hungry right now?" Peter stood and began to walk to the door. She had obviously lost her mind. "I need to go get help."

"Peter, you can't go get help. You're dead. Your humanness will fade away slowly. It takes about a day or so. They won't let you leave."

"Who? Who won't let me leave?" He put his hand on the doorknob.

"The inmates, the doctors, the nurses, they will all just bring you back in. I know; I tried." She continued twirling in her chair.

She has lost her mind. Or maybe I have. Peter pushed open the door to a brightly lit hallway abuzz with wandering patients, nurses, doctors, and orderlies. Regular hospital smells and sounds had replaced the empty, abandoned corridors. The bright electric lights blinded him. A nurse accosted him before he could step out of the room.

"Oh, Mr. Chancellor, you are just incorrigible. Please stay in the room. We will let you know when you can come out. Come on now, sir." She guided his arm back into the room and closed the door with a reassuring smile.

"Told ya so!" Angie stopped spinning and grinned at him.

Peter stood, unsure of what to do. He wanted to scream and cry and just lie down and sleep and hope it was all a bad dream. He looked over at Angie. "Angie, this might be your heaven," he looked doubtfully around him, "but it's not mine. Why am I here? What is going on?"

Angie rose from her chair and guided him to an army-like cot in the corner of the room. "Rest here and I will tell you what I know."

Stunned and zombie-like, he let her lead him to the cot while she pulled the chair over.

Angie began quietly. "First of all, they didn't do any bizarre torture treatments here, or satanic rituals or anything like that. These nurses and doctors all loved their patients. Especially in the last decade. In the early 80s, the state closed it down. There wasn't any money in the budget to keep it going. They moved the patients and locked up the building for good. The doctors moved on, the patients moved on, but they never found the same environment that they had here. So, as they died, they congregated here. This is *their* heaven. The sanatorium is a mixture of heavens. It is for the doctors and nurses who took care of patients and loved them, and for the patients who only felt love here. It became all of their heavens.

"When I pulled up, they knew I was Annabelle's daughter and that I was searching for answers. They knew the answers. I have them all, Peter. Some were even uglier than you were worried about. Some were beautiful. Peter, there is a reason you are here."

Peter's eyes could stay open no longer. He whispered, "Angie, I'm just so tired. Please just stop."

"You need to know. Peter, we are related, we..."

"Angie, please stop..."

"My mother was adopted. Her birth mother was young and pregnant and unmarried. She had twins. She gave my mother up and kept her sister. Stay with me, Peter..."

"No, I can't...I have to sleep..."

"There is more, so much more..."

The night continued outside the abandoned sanatorium. Time moved on all around, but inside, time stood still in a perfect harmony of life and death. The building seemed to sigh, grateful that the plan was in motion. A child's giggle floated away on the wind. He was planning, always planning.

Peter awoke to a dim grayish-green room with a small shaft of light coming from an oil-burning lantern sitting on a desk across the room. He swung his legs off the army cot and realized he didn't have his usual morning headache or stuffy nose. "I guess being dead does have some perks," he mumbled as he stood, expecting stiffness and sensing none.

"Yes, it does," Angie replied as she was enveloped in some ancient volume at the desk.

Peter pulled up a chair next to her. "I need some answers, Angie."

"I know," she sighed as she shut the dusty volume, "I'm not sure where to start." He noted a vulnerability in her attitude that he had never seen before. How could she just accept this? This was not his hell-fire Angela with her in-your-face attitude.

"Well, I know we are dead. I know almost everything about my mother from the time she was here until the time she died. I know what happened to her 'parents.' I know what happened to your mother and our grandmother." She stopped and looked down at her lap. The silence was uncomfortable.

"Okay, so, you know a lot. Good. What is it that you don't know?"

She shifted in her chair.

Peter turned her chair to face him. "Well, let me hit you with some of my own observations. First, I was not ready to be dead. I have a whole life to live. This is not fair. I didn't ask to be a part of your heaven and I don't want to be." Angie jumped as if he had physically hit her. "Second, I really don't think this is a 'good' thing. It's great that you have answers, but this place killed us." He stood up, waving his arms dramatically. "We wouldn't have died if that crazy nurse hadn't lured us in. So why is it good to be in a place that murdered us? I don't get it, Angie. I just don't get it." He sat back in the chair. "Have you been outside of this room?"

"No." She still wouldn't look up.

"So, we are not only freaking ghosts, but we are prisoners, also. Nice. What is it that you don't want to tell me? It can't be any worse than all of this."

"He killed us. My brother, Jacob. He was my twin and he was murdered. He has been planning his revenge all of this time."

Peter looked at her, blinked, and laughed. "Let me get this straight. A dead newborn orchestrated all of this," he waved his arms around again, "and now, what? Is he happy? Should we throw him a baby shower or something? Oh my God, Angie, this is all crazy. It's got to be a bad dream. I'm leaving. We're leaving. Besides, why would he want 'revenge' on us? We didn't do anything to him! We didn't kill him."

In a small wounded voice, she said, "He hates us. He hates us because we lived, and we were loved. He hates the town of Harmon Springs because they killed him. He hates my mother because she let him be murdered. His hate has become so powerful that he has been able to capture the lost souls of this ghostly place. The ghosts here are just wisps of what they were when they were alive. Some ghosts are stronger, like the head nurse and the doctors. Jacob is their leader."

"When you called to meet with the director, you were talking to a ghost then?" Peter asked.

She twisted in a dusty, upholstery-cracked chair. "If I were alive, I think I could faint dead away right now..."

"First of all, since when do you faint? You're talking crazy. We are leaving. I'm not going to just sit here. What can he do, kill me? I'm leaving, and you are coming with me. We are not dead." Angie sat like a stone statue. "Please, Angie, let's go."

"I don't know...I don't think I can..."

Peter grabbed her hands and pulled her up. "Yes, you can. Come on." He pulled her towards the door. He opened the door and once again, the hallway was abuzz with activity of a typical functioning hospital. There were no guards outside the door. Peter took the first step out of the room, pulling Angie behind him. The nurse appeared smiling.

"Oh! Mr. Chancellor and Miss Simpson! I am so happy that you are both feeling better. If you could just follow me, the doctor would like to have a word with you." Her voice was captivating and hypnotic. Peter looked back at Angie who was looking down the hallway where the nurse was headed. Without speaking, they both agreed to follow her. What else could the creepy nurse do to him, he reminded himself.

As they walked down the hallway, he whispered back to Angie, "Hey, is your mother here?"

"No, she moved on. But I don't know why; I thought that she would want to see me, or that she would feel like she had unfinished business."

"Shit," he hissed back to her, "I have unfinished business. My life - I can't believe this. Looks like she turned in there."

They stepped into a large open office, and a doctor greeted them. "Hello! I am so glad you could join us!" The doctor came around his desk, white garb flowing like a priestly robe. He grabbed Peter's hand and shook it vigorously and did the same with Angie. "Please, have a seat." They sat, unable to do anything else. "So, how has your stay been? Has the staff been accommodating?

Peter could only look at the doctor, unable to find the right words. Angie shifted in her seat, quiet. The doctor smiled encouragingly at them.

"I need to leave here," Peter started, "we need to leave here. We can't stay, we aren't..."

"Oh, my dear boy, no one wants to keep you here," the doctor said. "I was under the impression you needed information." This statement was directed at Angie.

"Yes," she replied, "we...umm...I need to know more about my mother."

Peter sighed. The doctor ignored him as he looked through some papers in an old, tattered folder. "Yes, Annabelle Mason. I trust you looked through her belongings." He was addressing Angie, but he was still looking at the papers.

"I did. But I was wondering about a few things. Did anyone..."

The doctor abruptly closed the file and cut her off impatiently. "Miss Simpson, you must understand that times were hard in those days. If you are here to file a lawsuit or to write up some sensational report for some news magazine, I must assure you that..."

"Oh, my God, no, no, that's not why we are here. I was just trying to find out what happened to her, how did she spend her days, who visited her, where is she buried..." Angie looked at her feet dejectedly.

Peter was appalled at her lack of 'hey, I'm in your face and you better listen to me' attitude, again. He addressed the doctor while looking at Angie with a questioning look. "Doctor. We don't want to sue, though now you make me think that something is going on here that we should be investigating. So, let's make a deal. You tell her what she wants to know, and we will leave and you will never hear from us again. Okay?"

The doctor appeared weary. "Annabelle never had any visitors. She spent her days drawing pictures of her daughter. She is buried out in the graveyard where we bury all of our patients who are unclaimed by relatives."

"But she did have relatives," Peter added in a whisper.

"Yes, we know, but they refused to take any responsibility for her, her bills, or her body. You have to understand that years ago, this was normal behavior. Families deposited mentally ill patients and forgot about them. They etched their names out of family trees and family Bibles." The doctor thumped the folder and began to hum an unrecognizable tune to himself.

"Okay, Angie, we have the information. Let's get out of here." Peter stood. Angie stood uncertainly. "What? Come on."

"I don't think we are done yet," she responded quietly.

"Oh, yes, we are." He grabbed her arm. The doctor turned in his swivel chair, awkwardly ignoring them, swinging his legs like a child.

Peter opened the door that led into the hallway. It was dark, moldy smelling and decayed. No hustle and bustle of a working hospital. "Angie, please tell me you are seeing this."

"Yes," she whispered, "Peter, we should leave. I agree. I think the main door is down that hallway. You go ahead. I need to go back to the records room and grab her things."

"Um. I don't know if you realize this, but when you are in a super scary place, you're not supposed to split up. Scary movies 10, sista."

She smiled, "I know, but it's on the way, I'll be right behind you. Don't forget about that rotted out hole by the front door. Besides we are dead, what can happen?"

"Okay, but you better be right behind me. I'm only going first so I can break through that front door in the most manly way possible."

"Thanks for being manly. Let's go."

Peter watched her look back into the doctor's office, then look back at him. He caught a glimpse of the doctor twirling in his swivel chair. "Let's go."

They felt along the wet, disintegrating walls. Angie turned into the records room, "I will be right there. Keep going."

Peter continued to feel his way down the hall. Short rays of light were gleaming through slats of the exterior windows. The hall was opening up to a foyer. He walked gingerly close to the wall, avoiding the open pit. He reached what he thought was the boarded-up door. There was just enough room to stand and push. He could feel the coolness of the pit creeping up his back. Poe described it perfectly. Hell, he's probably here somewhere. "Angie!" he yelled. "Hurry up!"

Down the hall, her voice echoed, "I'm coming!"

He shoved the door. It wasn't going to move. He stepped further over to the light beams coming through the slatted windows. He knew it would be a painful drop from the window, but a twisted or broken body part seemed like a fair deal to being dead. He reached the window and shoved a board. It didn't exactly fall from his touch, as much as it disintegrated at his touch. The light blinded him and he ducked his head back into the building. "Angie! Over here, come to the right when you get here. Hurry up!"

An echo down the hall, "Okay..."

"What? I can't hear you!" Peter tried to look out again. His eyes barely adjusted and he saw someone standing by his car. *Who the hell?* "There's someone out there Angie, come on."

He watched the figure move from his car to hers. Then the figure sat in her car. Damn it. He looked back, he couldn't see her, but he could hear her footsteps. "Someone's stealing your car. I'm going on out."

He jumped out of the window and felt the instant crunch of a bone breaking in his arm. Through the blinding pain, he stood and stumbled to Angie's car. "Hey, you...get out of that car." He was hoping to sound more menacing than he really did. Her car door opened. He limped up to the car and the figure emerged.

He stopped. He took inventory of his injuries; did he bump his head? He didn't remember hitting it. He stared.

Angie walked quickly to him. "Oh my God, Peter, what the hell happened to you? Why were you in that building?" She threw her cigarette down and went to steady him.

"No, no, don't grab my arm, it's broken. How did you get out here? Angie, there is no way. You were behind me."

Angie looked at him. "Peter, I don't know what you are talking about. How did you get in there? It's boarded up all around. Did you hit your head?"

She searched his head for bumps and his mind flashbacked to his foster mother who always checked him when he came in from a long day of playing with the kids on the block. He shook her off.

"I didn't hit my head, but I'm so confused. I followed you in there. The nurse showed me where you were...we talked to the doctor after you looked through your mom's things..."

Angie stopped him. "Peter. I did not go in there. When I pulled up, I tried to call the place again, but I had no cell phone service. I walked around the whole building looking for a way inside. I drove back to the restaurant to call you. But you didn't answer. It was dark, so I went back and got another night at the hotel. I figured I would try again this morning. So, I decided to go on to Harmon Springs, but at the last minute, I turned to come here. Then I came back around and saw your car. I called for you, and I had no idea where you could be. I knew you weren't in there, because there was no way inside. Or at least, I thought there was no way in. Peter, how did you get in there? What do you mean 'my mom's things'? Did you see my mom's things?"

Peter turned to look at the building. There was a nagging ache that he would see the other Angie peering at him at the broken window. But the widow was just an eyeless socket, impossibly high up. Damn, I fell a long way.

"Peter!" Angie turned him and he winced with pain. "Snap out of it! No, no, no...do not pass out!"

To his horror, he realized that was precisely what was happening. Peter felt the world slip away as he fell into nothing.

"God, Peter. Passing out is my job. Why do you always have to upstage me?" Angie broke his fall and laid him gently on the ground. She rummaged through her car and grabbed a jacket to prop his head. She slapped his face gently, though she wanted to hit harder. He'd obviously hit his head, but she didn't see any lumps or cuts. The sun was setting. "Come on, Peter. Wake up!" She slapped a bit harder, and he started to stir.

"Wow. Did I faint? Owww my arm!" He laid back down, gingerly.

"Come on, I am getting us out of here. How much gas do you have?"

"Kind of a personal question, don't you think?" He smiled.

"Okay, Mr. Delirious, how much gas is in your piece of crap car?"

"Hey, my car is not a piece of crap. It's almost on E," he added sheepishly.

"Fine. We are leaving your car and getting out of here. No arguments." She helped him up, and they moved towards her car.

"Did you hear that?" He stopped her from putting it in gear.

"Hear what? Peter, just buckle up. You need medical attention." She threw the car in reverse and he watched the building disappear in the dust. It was laughing he heard. A child's laughter. The child's laughter.

Chapter Twelve
Iron Rope Sanatorium
1974

A child's laughter,
Caught in the wind
Flows over and under the structures,
Long dead -
Follow it....

The night nurse walked importantly by the nurses' station. The young nurses were looking busy, but there was a sense of nonchalance about them. She could see that they were doing their job, but just the bare minimum. She knew that if she had walked by just ten minutes earlier, they would have been standing around laughing, joking, and not doing the job they were paid to do.

Her job was everything to her. This mental hospital was more than a job. Her family was very much a part of the hospital. Her mother had been a nurse before her, her father was a doctor, though long retired - both from the job and from life. Her younger sister was training to be a nurse. It is what her family did. They worked. They worked hard and they cherished this work.

She liked to begin each workday with a visit with her favorite patient. The women's wing was a joy for her. Most of the patients were unstable, mentally, and some physically. She felt that her strength was working with the female patients. It was common in the female portion of the hospital to have patients who were neither unstable nor ill. They were just victims of a corrupt system that gave them no voice. The female patients were victims of husbands who no longer needed or wanted them, or families that shunned them because they got pregnant too young and were unmarried.

She knocked lightly at the open door of Annabelle's room. "Good evening, Annabelle. How are you tonight?" She walked into the small room and found Annabelle sitting in the chair at her desk, drawing with the intensity of a child. "Oh, I see you are working at your drawing." She walked over to the table. She lightly touched the piles of single-leaf papers. All faces of the same young girl. The same face, over and over. "They are so lovely Annabelle. I think your Angel is so beautiful."

Annabelle stopped her furious drawing for a moment and then continued drawing.

"The doctor said that you are responding well to Lottie visiting. Maybe, you can start eating in the dining hall with the others or maybe even visit the grounds, and then you can make more friends like Lottie. You know Lottie had a child; I bet she misses him, also." She watched Annabelle shove the finished picture aside and grab another piece. "Well, sweetie, I'm going to make sure you have plenty of paper and charcoal. Can I get you anything else?"

Annabelle stopped again. She didn't look up, but a voice came from her lips, rusty and unused, "I miss her Nurse Timmons. I miss her."

Startled, but keeping her professional demeanor, the nurse put her hand on Annabelle's shoulder. "I know, sweetie. I know." Her own childless heart was breaking for Annabelle as she quietly left the room. She returned to her desk and wrote a note in Annabelle's file. "Patient is cooperative though still shows signs of mania. It is noted that she did speak tonight expressing a feeling of missing her one girl child." It wasn't unusual to have patients that have committed horrendous acts of violence. It wasn't her job to judge her patients. In her heart, she was sure that the State did the right thing and that "Angel" was safe in a loving, nurturing home. But there was that source of darkness that surrounded Annabelle. There was a baby boy that went missing and who was never found. She closed the folder and continued her night duties.

Chapter Thirteen

Harmon Springs
1963

The walls are the same
Every day
The windows, bars, are the same
Every day
The floors, hard, cold, are the same
Every day
The pain of something I can't have, is the same
Every day.

The mayor stepped into the sheriff's office. They both locked eyes for a moment. "Hey, why don't you close the door and have a seat." Clyde knew his friend. He knew that look. "What's going on, Ken?" He watched his usually self-assured, well-spoken friend fidget nervously.

"Remember when you came to ask me to do something about Annabelle and the babies?" Ken fidgeted and chewed a fingernail. It was odd-looking behavior for a grown man, but a habit he knew his friend suffered from.

"Yeah. You said you would take care of it." Clyde leaned back in his chair.

"There is something you need to know."

"Okay, I'm listening." Clyde was thankful the door was closed.

"I know that people are talking about her. I know that she can't raise those babies. But that isn't the issue I need to speak with you about." Ken stopped and looked at the floor.

Clyde remained silent. Ken continued to address the floor. "Those babies. I know who the father is."

Clyde sat up. "Why didn't you say so earlier? Who is it? Maybe we can find him and make him take the babies, or maybe we could..."

"No. No, friend. It's not that easy." Ken looked up. "They are my children."

Bile started building deep inside of Clyde. He knew his friend was serious. "You mean you...you and your daughter...Ken. What do you mean?" Even as he asked, he knew. He knew of Ken's weakness for female companionship. He knew that Clarisse had no use for marital relations. He knew as long as he'd been Ken's friend, he'd been his clean up man. He had helped Ken out of many a precarious situation with many a different girl. Ken did not answer. "My God, Ken. She is your daughter. How could you? Why? Why didn't you come to me? We could have found someone for you in another town...someone not RELATED to you?!" Ken winced.

"She is not related to me, remember?" Ken muttered.

Clyde stared at Ken. Indecision made him hesitate. He spoke, but his voice didn't seem to be his own. "Yes. Yes, she is. She is the product of one of your affairs."

It was Ken's turn to be surprised. "What the hell? What do you mean? I thought some teenage girl in trouble..." and then it made sense. It was a girl in trouble. A girl that agreed to spend a weekend with Ken and Clyde.

"Why didn't you tell me? Don't you think I had the right to know that she was my own flesh and blood? Why would you keep that from me?"

"Look. I had my reasons. The important question here is: what the hell are you gonna do? You've not only committed incest, but there were children produced. It never occurred to me that you would be tempted by your own child, whether she was blood or not."

"Don't judge me. I tried not to. I was drinking. She was there. It was easy. No one cares about her. Everyone just sees her as that 'poor retarded girl.' Now it's all just a mess." He hung his head.

"Does Clarisse know?"

"No. And she won't know. God. What have I done? Clyde. You have to help me. Just this one last time. You have to help me. If she finds out, it will devastate her. God, not to mention the fact that she is really...oh my God..." He stood abruptly and threw up in the wastebasket by the desk.

Clyde sat contemplating the heaving man. "Well, it's nice to see you have some guilt about it, but I'm not judging you. Hell, I was just as guilty as you."

Ken wiped his mouth on his sleeve. "Man, you got to help me."

"What exactly do you want me to do? I can't exactly turn back time or anything."

"I don't know. Can't we move her and the ...babies...away from here? Or maybe we could kill them..." Ken's eyes reflected the wildness of a desperate man.

"Good God, Ken. You've gone crazy."

"This is your mess too. Even if there is no 'proof,' you were still there. You also partook of the festivities. If you don't help me, I'll be ruined. I'll never get voted back in, or be able to hold my head up in town. Clarisse will be ruined. It will be too much for her to take."

"Why don't we just sit back and stay quiet. No one knows anything but us. If we don't say anything, then no one will know. Wait. Annabelle. I guess she would know?"

"No, she thinks angels impregnated her."

"Angels?"

"Yeah, I drugged her, so she wasn't seeing things too clearly."

"You really needed it that bad? You took advantage of a mentally ill girl that was in your care?"

"I was weak. I was drunk. I have a problem."

"If you were drunk, then how did you think to drug her? Sounds kinda premeditated to me."

Ken didn't answer.

"You are a monster."

"I know. I'm so sorry." Ken began to cry. Through his strangled sobs, he sputtered, "We could make it look like an accident, a fire, they wouldn't suffer. The smoke will kill them first. Everyone would believe it since they know she is feeble-minded."

"It won't be that easy. And what about Clarisse? Don't you think she will be devastated about losing her daughter and her grandchildren...which are really her stepchildren..." Clyde's stomach rolled. He kept an eye on the waste paper basket.

"Yes, yes," Ken sobbed, "she will be devastated, but I think she'll be relieved, too. She is just as concerned about Annabelle's future, and the future of those babies."

"So, in other words, it's not really about Clarisse or Annabelle or the babies. It's really about you."

"No, no, I'm trying to fix this for all of us."

"Okay, humor me. What is your plan?"

"Fire. Her place is a mess. A freak fire would be believable. They would all die, and this will all be over."

"Ken, this is crazy. You are asking me, your friend, to not only break the law – remember, I am the sheriff – but more specifically, you want to kill three human beings. How can you think this is okay? I'm not going to do this. It's wrong. Let's just be patient and let it work out."

"Clyde. You will do this for me. Remember, I have the power to take you out of this job. And maybe your wife would like to know about some of your own excursions." Clyde did not miss the hint of evil in his friend's voice.

"Oh, so it's blackmail then? I'm shocked to be blackmailed by such a stand-up kind of guy. Go, get the hell out of here. I will call you later. I need to process." He swiped his face in frustration. Ken was still sitting there. "Get out now," Clyde growled.

Ken stood, sweaty, and nervous as he left the office.

Clyde stood and kicked at his chair. He did love his wife and he knew that Ken had a ruthless streak. All politicians did, in his mind. He knew that Ken would betray him. He did feel responsible for this mess. He had been trying to fix it since Annabelle was born.

The "girl in trouble" lived in Bardstown, not too far from Harmon Springs. He learned of her from a fellow sheriff from that town. He had mentioned to Clyde that there was a young girl who was willing to work her way through traffic tickets and other misdemeanor offenses. One thing led to another and before long, Clyde had arranged a weekend with the young lady. This was normal business for Clyde. He often helped Ken with his sexual appetite. He benefited as well. It was invigorating to have the attention of a young girl with no sexual hang-ups.

That weekend they were both supposed to attend a symposium on drugs and alcohol upstate. Both wives packed their husbands' bags for the weekend with love and care.

The men drove to the outskirts of Bardstown. The girl's house was on a dead-end street. All weekend they took turns at the girl, who was more than eager for the company. Everyone was a consenting participant. Everyone got what they wanted. Only later, nine months later, the girl called with the news.

"I'm pregnant. I need help," she said.

"I told you not to contact me." As he was speaking quickly into the phone, he noted that his office door was slightly ajar. He hoped his secretary couldn't hear him.

"I'm having a baby, and you will help me –"

"Listen, who knows how many men you've been with. Stop calling – "

"No. You are wrong. One of you is the father and I need help. I wasn't with anyone during that time but you two." There was a silence on the line. "Did you hear me? I need help."

"I don't know what you want me to do? This is your problem, I, we don't – "

"You don't understand *Sheriff*. If you don't help me, I will expose both of you for the monsters you are. Won't your wives be surprised – "

With his eyes on his door, he told her that he would call her back with a plan. When he set the phone down, he felt dirty. Yes, he thought his wife would be surprised if he fathered a child. The doctor fixed him with a snip after the birth of his son. But Clarisse, yes, she would be surprised and devastated. The whole town knew how much she wanted to have a child. What a blow to find out that her husband fathered one with a young girl in another town.

He came up with the plan. He would take the baby to Ken and Clarisse to raise. He wouldn't tell Ken because he didn't want Ken to be reminded of his infidelity every time he looked at the child. This young mother did not want to be a mother and so it seemed to make sense for all involved. Ken's legitimate fatherhood would stay a secret that he would have to keep.

The Sheriff traveled back to Bardstown. Alone this time, he traveled down the dead-end road and knocked on that same door. The girl answered the door and led him to the same front room they both had sex with her in when they first arrived, within the first ten minutes. Now, she was tired, maybe drained by the birthing process, maybe by something else. The newborn was packed and ready to go. The girl didn't seem upset or happy about giving up the child. It was almost like it was just a routine thing that she had to deal with.

"Here," he handed her an envelope of papers, "sign these. They ensure that you won't come trying to get parental rights or anything like that." He stood, holding them out to her. She didn't react at first. Then she snatched them out of his hand.

"I will sign your damn papers. Then get the hell out. I ought to make you sign some damn papers saying you raped me." She signed the papers.

"We didn't rape you. You were paid. You were willing." He felt a surge of heat and hoped she could not his sweat.

She handed the papers to him. "Yeah. Okay. Take the baby and get out of my house."

He lifted the baby basket and left her house. His heart was uneasy and his mind was unsure. It just felt wrong, but he couldn't pinpoint why.

She stood in her doorway and watched him pull away in his cruiser. With a confident smile, she shut the door. She walked to the back room to console her other baby. The sheriff did not know, and he would never know, that she delivered twins. He did not know and he would never know that the cycle of retribution had begun.

Chapter Fourteen

Chicago
1985

She doesn't want to be alive anymore
She enslaves others around her
Her twins separated at birth
She waits for the resolution

"Let's make s'mores!" Peter jumped up to look through her cabinets. "One thing I know for sure Angie, s'mores make studying so much better." He shuffled through cabinets. "Girl, you know that as a woman, you are supposed to have s'mores ingredients on hand at all times."

Angie waved off his comment, "yeah, well, I guess my mom left that out of my education on how to be a woman."

Peter continued searching for ingredients. "You know, you should be happy you were adopted by a loving family. Trust me, growing up in the system was rough. But look at me now! My last year of college, a promising career in store, and a gorgeous body to entice the boys with." He grabbed a mixing bowl.

"Yes, it is obvious you survived and you are not too screwed up." She was looking doubtfully at him as he was mixing peanut butter, butter, chocolate chips, brown sugar, and marshmallows together. "Maybe I should take that back..."

"It'll be good, trust me!" He waved his arms flamboyantly and then continued mixing. "You don't talk too much about your family. You always listen to my drama." He divided the mixture into two bowls and added spoons. They walked back into the front room of the small dorm apartment. He offered her a bowl with a self-satisfied grin.

"What is it?" she pushed the cookie dough-like mixture around the bowl.

"I call it, "My Favorite Thing." Try it!" His eager face made her smile. She took a tentative bite. Pure sugar. She was sure that she was going to get instant diabetes.

"It's good."

"You are so lying! It's okay. It will grow on you. Okay, now for the rest of the night, we are talking about you. It's the Angie Show! So, what were they like, your parents?"

"I guess anything is better than doing this paper on Chaucer." She rolled her eyes. "Okay, well, they were quiet. They were very much down to earth, simple. Not complicated. I don't remember much about the small town we are from, just the name, Harmon Springs. They said they were forced to move when the mill closed. Shortly after the mill closed, a new highway was built that rerouted traffic away from the town. So, they packed us all up and moved here to the Chicago land area. There's lots of steelwork here." She took another bite.

"You have brothers and sisters? I didn't know that! You've never said anything about them."

"I guess it never came up. They were okay. They just made sure that I always remembered my place and that I was not a real 'part' of the family. I think they resented me. Because of me there was one less piece of chicken, on less present at Christmas and birthdays, that kind of thing.

"It's no big deal really," she continued. "I just always wondered about my real parents. What happened to them, why did they give me up, you know, the same thing all adopted kids think about."

Peter snorted, "Well, not all of them. I know what happened to my mom. She was an addict, in and out of jail. Foster homes were not the best places to be, but at least I knew I would get food and a warm place to sleep. I never knew that with my mom. I remember waiting for her in the dark; I was hungry, dirty and sick. It may have been days. Who knows? The state finally found me, I don't know how; some neighbors maybe? But hey, I'm taking over again. Sorry." He smiled.

Angie smiled back at him. "I expected it, Mr. Center of Attention."

"I am a drama queen, I must admit." He took another spoonful of the sweet, gooey mess. "Didn't you say once that someone had told you that your real mom was institutionalized?"

"Yes, actually, it was one of my brothers. He was teasing me one day, saying my mom was living in a nut house. My adopted mom overheard, I guess. She came running into the room and smacked him hard across the face. He really hated me after that day. You know, all I wanted was to feel like I fit in; that I was wanted."

"Yeah, me too."

"Anyway, I don't know if it was true. But looking back now, it might have been. I don't think she would have reacted like that if it wasn't. It's not like she would protect me for just nothing. Does that make sense?"

"Yes," he scooped another bite.

"How are you not fat?" she eyed him enviously as he ate the sugary mixture. She felt like each bite she took cemented itself to her outer thighs.

He shrugged, "I work out. You should join me sometime...we could..."

"Umm no. Working out messes up my cigarette habit," she laughed.

They shoved their bowls aside and sat back in quiet sugar bliss.

Peter sat up. "Angie, I have an idea."

Angie lit a cigarette already knowing what he was going to say. "Oh yeah?"

"Yes. What if we look for your parents? I have the skills, you know."

Angie considered it for a moment. "I dunno, Peter. It would be a lot of work. I really wouldn't even know where to start. Besides, I don't have time and you don't either. This is our last semester and then we are off into the work world."

Peter agreed and conversation turned to cute guys and possibilities of serious hookups in the future.

Chapter Fifteen
Iron Rope Sanatorium
1974

How can I tell her
How much I loved her?
I can show her
Through poems
Through drawings,
Through art.
It is the only truth.

"Doctor, I have a question if you have a moment." Nurse Timmons sat next to him in the small-designated eating area. It was rare when the director of the hospital was alone, and she grabbed the moment. He merely motioned for her to sit and continued eating.

"Would you consider letting Annabelle Mason have some time out in the Reflection Garden grounds?"

He flinched at the sound of her name but made no other motion to acknowledge the request.

"Sir, she is doing very well. I feel like she would benefit from some sunshine and..."

"So, you presume to know how to treat her more than I do? Maybe you should be the head physician here then." He threw his fork down.

"No, no Doctor Snellin, I am sorry. I've overstepped my boundaries," she acquiesced, but she didn't move.

He threw his napkin on his tray. "Put your recommendation on her chart." He stood, "Excuse me," and he left the dining area.

The nurse left the dining area with a sense of purpose. She would get Annabelle out of her room. It was her goal, and she never gave up on a goal.

Doctor Snellin walked quickly down the back hallway that led to his office. He nodded curtly at staff that he passed. When the door of his office closed behind him, he exhaled as if for the first time. His legs were weak and sweat was now beading down the sides of his face. He half stepped, half fell to his desk. Using his arms, he pushed himself around it to sit in his large, 'I'm the boss here' chair. He fumbled the bottom drawer open and pulled out the container. The white powder screamed at him. As he scratched out the lines, he thought of Annabelle Mason. He was a young doctor when he was first assigned to her. He remembered those first meetings, before her lobotomy. He made mistakes. He was young. Inexperienced. It was a power trip. He was ruled by lust. Lust of power and control. Just as his guilt was manifesting, the drug took hold and he sat back in his bliss.

Chapter Sixteen
Bardstown
1960

The mother watches the spiral
The downward spiral
Of her daughter
Powerless,
Impotent
She reaches out
But it is too late.

Janelle opened the door. "What the hell do you want?" She sneered at the man holding a hat and not making eye contact with her. She walked back to her Lazy Boy, leaving him at the door. He stepped in. He stood uncomfortable.

"I need some information."

She huffed and lit a cigarette. "You give me $20 and I will tell you whatever you want me to." She laughed and coughed. The years had not been kind to her, and she had not been kind to herself. When she was younger, she was a "looker." She had no problems attracting and using men. Then things began to change. She tried a drug, and then another, and then another. She added alcohol. She liked them all and she worshiped them. She was already on her downward spiral the weekend her twin girls were conceived. This man took one of them, starting her cycle of revenge.

Now, years later, she wished he'd taken the other one also. At first, she thought it might be okay to have a child. She had only needed the one to start the cycle and was pleased when she found out that she was having twins. However, the kid held her back and made her feel old. She did not want to stay home all the time with the brat. She wanted to go party with friends. Now she broiled in hate, fueling the revenge for what they did to her, the men and the kids. But right now, her only concern was her next fix.

She often left the baby alone in the house. She would stumble home half-blind from drinking and drugs and find that the brat had pulled out food from the cabinets. Rice was dumped all over the floor. Little kid footprints were all over the house because she got into the flour. Keeping the kid was a decision she regretted.

She beat the girl all the time. For any reason. She got high and beat her because she asked about dinner. She got drunk and beat her because she wanted a drink of water. She beat her because she kept getting sick with colds and fevers.

She took another drink of her vodka and tea mixture. "What do you want Mr. Sheriff? Hurry up, I got company comin' and he pays more than you ever did."

Clyde cleared his throat. "When you were pregnant with Annabelle, were you using?"

She laughed. "What do you care? You guys got what you wanted. What the hell did I get?" She noted that he would not look at her. "Yeah, I was using. I was high on everything I could find. While you guys were laughing it up in one room, I went in the next room and shot up my drugs and drank whiskey to chase it down. I was feeling good." She smiled at the thought of her time before kids. She could get as high as she wanted, party when she wanted, no one to cry and whine about food and whatever else they thought they needed.

Sherriff Harrison looked at her closely. Her face was old, yellow, and sunken. Her hair was thin and falling out. Her teeth, what were left of them, were blackening.

She smiled evil and slow. "Like whatcha see Mr. Sherriff Man? You want some more? I can give you a good discount. Yes, sir." She laughed. "Why you want to know what I was on? Is that brat I gave you messed up or somethin'? I hope so. I hope she is miserable. I want everyone to be miserable, just like me. Now get the hell out of my house. I got company comin' and I ain't got no time for no man who ain't payin'."

He put on his hat. "She is beautiful. Just in case you wanted to know."

"Good. Send her back on home; I will put her to work. The only good job round here is whorin'. Send her on this way." She laughed at him, a mixture of hideous cackling and emphysema hacking.

Clyde turned and left her house. He didn't return. He found out what he needed to know. Annabelle could have possibly suffered from some fetal drug addiction or suffered some damage in the womb. That could be why she was the way she was. Different. As he drove away, he had the urge to bathe.

In the upstairs window, a young girl watched him drive away. She was cutting her arm. She concentrated on the little cuts. They were bright red and then turned dark brown as blood welled along the strip of pain. She looked back out of the window and watched the dust fall back into place. The client was due any moment. She needed to be ready. Her mother made sure that she performed appropriately. All money went to her mother. If she did not perform, she did not eat. Her mother kept her weak so she could not run away. One thing her mother did not know was that her period had not started this month. She completed a few more cuts and then she heard her mother's footsteps on the stairs.

"Whore. You better be ready. What you doin'?" She stood at the girl's door with her hands on her hips.

"Nothin' mother. I'm ready." The young girl stood, too thin, she stumbled a bit and then followed her mother down the stairs. The client was on his way. Her mother would watch the entire transaction to make sure no extra money was given and to make sure that the girl did her job.

"Mother, I'm hungry." She whispered.

The woman slapped her across the face. "You whore. You'll eat when you earn yur keep. You ruined my life. You deserve to starve a little. If I could, I kill you where you stand for all the hell you've caused me, I would believe you me. But you make me money right now. If that ends, you end." She was in the girl's face, spitting vileness.

The girl arranged herself on the couch. The knock sounded at the door. Her 'date' was here. He stepped into the room. He was an old regular. The girl hated this particular old man. His appetite was insatiable and of all her 'dates,' he made her feel the dirtiest. He smiled a wolf grin at the girl. She could see him already devouring her.

This was perfect for him. He got to take advantage of this young girl who looked so much like his beautiful daughter and he had an audience, which turned him on even more. He liked his time with

Lottie, and he paid a lot of money for her. His deal was that he paid enough to keep Lottie for himself.

Her mother, who was once a conquest of his, broke his reverie.

"Get your clothes off bitch, what are ya waitin' for. We ain't got all day." She moved over to her easy chair to watch the man sexually assault her daughter, and, as always, she got her revenge every time because he didn't know he was assaulting his own daughter. There you go, Mr. Mason. You just keep up the cycle. They were both paying for ruining her and she was being paid for watching it, and she would have the money for at least the next couple fixes. It was perfect. It was even more perfect when her daughter cried softly as he used her the way he wanted, whatever his money would cover.

"You just stay your ass here and when you deliver that evil baby, you go to hell. I'm done with you." Lottie's mother left her at the small hospital and never saw her again. Lottie delivered a healthy baby boy. The nurses were sympathetic. It was hard for them to watch the drama unfold. They watched the patient's mother stomp out of the hospital.

The new mother held her baby boy. She was sixteen. The nurses also did not miss the scars on the young woman's arms and legs. Lottie looked up at the nurse who was adjusting the IV. "What am I going to do now?"

The nurse shrugged sadly. "You can go to the home for unwed mothers. It's in the city. We are looking into a place for you there. I'm so sorry we don't have more to offer you."

Lottie hugged her baby close to her. She whispered into his perfect little ear. "I promise to take care of you and do right by you. I won't be like my mom. I will make sure you have better. I promise." The baby yawned a big baby yawn and snuggled into her breast.

She was able to stay for a bit at the shelter but soon fell into hanging with friends that she could never have before. Those friends were free and easy with drugs and alcohol. She started prostituting again, but she kept the money this time.

She was a terrible parent. All she wanted was not to be a mother. Her son often went hungry and cried. She beat him if she was home, but she wasn't home often. One day she came home to two people in suits trying to stand in the living room. It was an insane mess. The two-year-old boy was dirty, naked, and laying on a pile of filth, listless. Body lice were crawling on him and he had sores that were open and oozing. Lottie was too messed up to see how serious the situation was.

Her speech was slurred, "What the hell are you doin' in my house...get out of here." She stumbled towards the bedroom. She just wanted to lie down. She walked a couple of steps and passed out, falling on the floor. The child cried and ran to her. The Child Protective Service workers looked at each other.

"Grab the child. I will take care of the paperwork. Let's get out of here." They picked up the weakly sobbing boy and left the house. The boy was still crying when they put him in the car. One of the workers put her hand on his head. He ducked instinctively. She jerked her hand back.

"How old are you, little guy?"

"I two. I two. I two. I two." He cried.

"Well, Mr. Two-year-old, we are going to take you somewhere and feed you. Are you hungry?"

"I hungry! I hungry!" He cried weakly.

"Okay, okay," she smiled at him. The driver looked at her through the rearview mirror. They knew the danger. Before they walked into the house, her fellow social worker reminded her of rule number one: Don't become attached to the children. It was hard. They were always so wounded, so needy. It was a long drive back to town. The child was asleep by the time they arrived.

Chapter Seventeen
Iron Rope Sanatorium
1975

The abandoned life
Curls inside to comfort itself
In the destroyed world
Of dreams

Lottie gathered her slippers so that she could go visit her good friend Annabelle. Annabelle was the only person in the hospital that she felt she could trust, and that she liked to talk to. Annabelle was different. Though Annabelle didn't speak very much, Lottie kept up the conversation just fine. She had been drug and alcohol free for years. Regular food and sanitary conditions were good for her. She regretted losing her boy, but she knew now that it was the best for him. The days after losing him were blurry, but she had moments of clarity. She remembered standing on a street flashing passersby. Then there was a jail stay. Then there was Iron Rope. Annabelle had lost a child also. They had that in common, as well as questionable reasons why they were patients at the sanatorium.

"Hey Annabelle, how are you today?" Lottie strolled into her room. Annabelle smiled shyly. "I hear that old Mr. Johns is running down the halls naked again. Isn't that hilarious!" She looked at Annabelle's latest artwork. "Oh, you are so good at this. I'm so envious. I can't draw nuthin'." She held up the charcoal drawing of the baby girl's face that she had grown to know. It was Annabelle's Angel. "Aww, she is so pretty. She reminds me so much of my son. He had such a sweet face. Then, I don't know. Then I got all messed up. It's like I remember him when he was a little newborn, but then, when the drugs took hold, I don't know, I just can't remember nuthin'. I like it here though. Regular food, good friends," she nudged Annabelle, "and some not so ugly male workers, eh?"

Annabelle put her hand on Lottie's shoulder. She whispered, "I miss her."

After the visit, Annabelle put her pictures away and arranged her blankets. She listened to the sound of the night shift moving along in the building. The sounds of patients crying, laughing, quietly talking, all blended together.

"Annabelle, wake up. It's time for your medicine and I have a surprise for you." The orderly handed Annabelle the pills and took the bedpan to the hallway cart. He placed a clean one next to her bed and handed her a small cup with water to wash the pills down. "Good job, Annabelle. The night nurse and the doctor both agree that you should get some time outside today. Isn't that great news?" He smiled at her. She looked ahead blankly. Unlike some of the other patients, she functioned relatively normally; she just didn't speak or respond in anyway.

He looked around her room. "Annabelle, I have a confession to make. I'm sure you won't mind." He helped her lay back down on her clean sheets. "Yes, I know you are sleepy now, but just bear with me. The pills are taking effect; that is why you can't hold your eyes open. I just wanted you to know that I'm sorry. When the good doctor presented the opportunity, well, I had to go along with it. My wife is having our sixth child and we just ain't got enough money for carin' for all of them children. But, now, because I did this service for the doctor, we're set for a long while. I know you won't mind. It may just ease your pain to sleep awhile. Right? I'm sorry you won't get to see outside too. He touched her face. "Oh, you are already gone. Okay, good lady. No one will be in until lunchtime, so you will not be saved. God bless."

The orderly left the room with a heavy heart, heavier than he thought it would be. His heavy heart could not override the relief he felt not to have to hear his children cry from hunger anymore. No one would miss Annabelle Mason. That is what the doctor said. The orderly continued his daily duties, though not in the high spirits he thought he would be feeling.

Nurse Timmons stood in the morgue, looking at the long line of cold metal tables. Some held bodies, some sat empty and gleaming in the laboratory light. She was looking for one.

"Well, hello there Nurse Timmons. How can I help you?" The mortician acknowledged her as he was wiping his hands with a towel. "This is not part of your usual rounds, is it?" he asked curiously.

She dismissed his curiosity with and nod and replied, "I am looking for Annabelle Mason. She died earlier this..."

"Yes, this morning. She's over here. Right this way." As he walked along the tables, he thought that it was not good business to become close to the patients. In his years here, he had seen it happen more than not. Nurses, orderlies, cafeteria workers, and even doctors sometimes sought out patients after death to say some sort of private goodbye. Death was a natural part of life and was his business, but it was hard when you let the patients get too close.

"Here she is." He double-checked the paperwork on her table; he was a very thorough man. He stood, unsure of what to do next. Was she here to evaluate his work? He slowly uncovered the patient's face. He knew that Nurse Timmons was known for her hardness and matter-of-fact way, so he was confused as he watched the tough night nurse look down at Annabelle Mason. Her eyes were sad, not tear-filled, not even red, just sad. She covered the woman's face. At that moment, he knew that her visit had nothing to do with him, and everything to do with this patient.

She didn't look away from the shrouded body as she asked, "Did Dr. Snellin order an autopsy?"

"No, why would he? It was a heart attack. He examined her himself."

"Thank you." She turned and walked out of the morgue.

The mortician watched her leave. In another time, in another world, he might have stopped her. He might have explained that it was no heart attack and he knew it. There was nothing physically wrong with the woman. He knew a great many secrets held in the institution because he dealt with the deaths. Sometimes the deaths were natural, sometimes they were suicides, and sometimes they were murder. Dr. Snellin controlled everything, up to and including who lived and died.

The mortician turned to look at the woman lying on the table. He had no idea what she had done, but he suspected she was in a better place. He caught a movement in the corner of his eye, turned quickly, but nothing was there. He shrugged, not being a man who was easily spooked and resumed his duties.

Nurse Timmons entered Annabelle's room, which was still untouched. Quietly, efficiently, she began packing Annabelle's things. She picked up Annabelle's last drawing of her "Angel." A beautiful baby girl. She folded the drawing carefully and tucked it into her pocket. "I will not let this go, Annabelle. I will find out what happened to you. I promise."

"Well, that is rather dramatic, don't you think?" Dr. Snellin stepped closer to her. She didn't answer him and put her hand protectively on the box that held what was left of Annabelle. "You know, it doesn't do any good to become attached to them. They are barely human and certainly not curable." He sniffled and coughed into a handkerchief. "You are my best nurse; I need your talents and sensibility with the patients who are alive. Nothing *happened* to her Nurse Timmons. She died. They do that. They die. And *we* will die someday. This room is already reserved for another patient who needs room and board. I suggest you let her go. Times are too hard right now to be without work, don't you agree?" he added deliberately.

"Yes, sir. I will put these in the records room." She didn't miss the acid venom in his tone or the barely veiled threat. As she walked out of the room, she wondered at herself. *Was it age? Was it exhaustion?* Why did she not fight back, push against his cold hate and defend Annabelle? Her position as the head Night Nurse was a cherished one. For twenty years, she cared for her patients, taught new nurses, and made sure that her watch ran smoothly. She was all rules and regulations, and people were now reduced to numbers? Files? Cases? Money.

Annabelle surprised her. Annabelle was different. She felt that it was unfortunate that Annabelle was institutionalized. In her first years, she would have stood up to him. In her first years, she vocalized her opinions and observations. In her early years, she would have stood up to his threat of taking her job. Years ago, she would have told him that she was suspicious of him. But now, she just accepted it and moved along, like everyone else. She was tired. It was too late for Annabelle, maybe too late for all of them. Nurse Timmons could smell the corruption at the seat of her hospital as well as the bleach cleaner that was a staple in everyday life at Iron Rope. As she walked by the nurse's station, she overheard snippets of conversations.

"I think he has it."

"Did you hear him coughing?"

"No, I didn't see any blood, but that doesn't mean..."

"There is something wrong with..."

"Ladies. Can we begin our rounds, or are we going to stand around and gossip all night?" Nurse Timmons looked sternly at the young nurses who all hung their heads as they grabbed charts and moved to their rounds. So, they had suspicions, also. However, theirs were not about what happened to Annabelle, and the doctor's corruption, but about the doctor and his health. Contracting tuberculosis was a fear that many health workers faced.

The institution had gone through many stages throughout the years. When she started, Iron Rope housed mentally ill people, most of whom had no money or family. Later the patients they received were more criminally insane, and two other wings had to be added on for housing them. Then, there was a slow progression of poor degenerates who had no other place to go, children with no parents, children born to patients. Now, the great illness. Tuberculosis was like the plague. No one wanted the afflicted around, so they sent the afflicted from all the surrounding counties to Iron Rope.

Nurse Timmons opened the door to the records room, walked along the shelves, and deposited the box in the "M" section. Too many boxes. Too many deaths. She did not have the strength to fight Dr. Snellin directly, but there were other ways.

She turned off the light and continued with her duties. It was going to be a long double shift. She needed to ask the morning orderly some pointed questions, although in her heart and intuition, she already knew the answers.

"Nurse Timmons. Are we short staffed this morning?" the Head Nurse smiled politely, confused and instantly on edge at the sight of the Night Nurse brandishing a clipboard.

"No, no, I just needed to pick up a shift for the holidays. Times are hard." She sounded more convincing than she thought she would.

"Oh, yes, I totally understand. I love how you think ahead. Christmas is months away." The Head Nurse exhaled, relieved. Evaluations could happen anytime; it was one more stress that the workers had to face on top of their regular duties.

"Yes," Nurse Timmons agreed, clutching the inventory clipboard, "I'm just going to catalog the new shipment of medications. Please don't let me keep you."

"That will be wonderful. Thank you so much. It'll certainly free up two nurses, and today is a heavy day with seven new patients. Six of them are positive for TB." The day nurse shook her head and returned to her plans for her nurses for the day. "I will just make some changes here and here..."

Nurse Timmons turned away, headed for the linens closet. The orderly should be there gathering clean linens for his rounds. She had forgotten how bright the hallways were with the natural light coming in. There was something comforting about working the night shift, almost like it was her world, and she was in charge, protected by darkness all around. Dayshift was strange, open, almost pleasant, which was a false hope in this place.

She walked into the linen's closet and he was there, piling them up on his cart. "Hello, Benjamin."

He started and turned at the sound of his name. "Heck, you scared me, Nurse Timmons. Hello. What brings you here this mornin'?" He nervously touched the sheets on his cart, almost as if to say, 'I'm just doing my job here.' He was thirty-two years old, but she always made him feel like a young, errant teenager.

"I just wanted to ask you about something if you have a moment." She helped him push his cart out of the closet and they walked together in the hallway.

He hesitated a fraction of a moment. She could see him trying to connect reasons why. "Oh, sure, anything for you, missus. You know I'm always thankful to you for helpin' me get this job. It's been a Godsend to me and the family. That's for sure." They entered the first room, empty. He spread the sheet and she helped him gather the ends.

"I want to ask you about Annabelle Mason." She saw something dart behind his eyes, but he continued intently making up the bed for a new patient.

"Yeah, she passed the other day, right?" She could see him trying to act casual.

"Yes, she died of a heart attack."

"Yup, such a shame. She was a good lady. She never gave me no trouble."

"Did she act strangely that morning; anything different?" She handed him the heavy wool blanket to help spread it on the bed.

"Well, I reckon not. I don't recall. She was gone when they came in at lunch. I reckon I was the last to see her alive. So sad."

"I just wanted to check; it just seemed so sudden. Thank you Benjamin, you have a great rest of your shift."

"Thank you. The wife is havin' another baby any day now. Times is scary with all this lung disease out there. People are hungry, I tell ya. Sometimes I wonder if being dead isn't just an easier way ta go. You know?"

"I understand. Life is hard, but every new child is another chance to bring some hope in the world. Maybe your new one will find the cure for TB or for some other godforsaken illness."

"Let's hope we don't have to wait that long." He patted the bed. "Nothin' like a clean, crisp bed." He smiled and headed for the mop water.

"Okay, I'm going to go log in the new meds. Thank you. Have a great day."

"You too, Nurse Timmons." He watched her leave the room and his smile turned down to concern. *Did she know? Was I convincing?* He mopped without thinking of mopping. He was thinking of his family. Dr. Snellin had it covered, he knew. He knew he had sold his soul to the devil, but it was for his family; surely, God would understand. As he swiped the floor, the brown water in the bucket rippled.

Chapter Eighteen
Iron Rope Sanatorium
June 12, 1975

Hate grows and builds
Worlds – worlds beholden to it
The cycle feeds
And feeds
Until
Hate has no more fuel
No more power – then
What replaces it?

The days are growing longer and harder to face without it. I cannot function without it. The staff is growing suspicious of me. I can deny it for only a short time more. I am taking the drug more than three times a day. I cannot get enough. I cannot sleep without it, I cannot wake without it, I cannot work without it. I am its slave. My days are coming to an end. I have done some terrible things in my life, but I hope that I am remembered for the good that I accomplished. This godforsaken institution has grown and prospered under my care. I have helped more patients than I've hurt. Lord, save my soul.

Dr. Snellin closed his journal. He tucked it away in the same drawer as the drug. His hand lingered over the ornately ornamental box that contained his salvation. Instead, he reached for the other box. He opened the latch and pulled out the pistol. He could do it. He should do it. He wrapped his finger around the trigger. With a sob, he thrust the pistol back in the box.

He gathered the other box and snorted himself into oblivion. Darkness crept into the room. His head rested on his desk. His mouth was slack with drool making a puddle, muddled by the fine white powder residue on the desk. A small hand, an impossibly small hand covered his nose and mouth.

Nurse Timmons knocked quietly on the doctor's door. She would just tell him that she had some concerns about Benjamin and that maybe Annabelle's death needed to be investigated. Though she knew the doctor was the real murderer, she needed a way to show him that she not only knew, but that she was actively pursuing the case of Annabelle's death. Her shift was technically over, but this just couldn't wait.

She knocked again. She knew he was in there because his car was still out front. "Sir," she tried the doorknob. "Sir, may I have a moment?" She opened his door and saw him lying on the floor. She ran to him and instinctively listened for breathing. As soon as she touched his cold skin, she knew he was dead. She noted the powder on his nose. The remains of the powder scattered on the desk told its own story.

She made a rash decision. She needed to protect the hospital. She quickly cleaned up the mess and then wiped his face. Once the evidence was disposed of, she called for help.

His death certificate would say he died of a heart attack. She half-smiled at the justification of it all. She called in help, knowing it was too late.

******

Ghosts of lives floated through the abandoned hallways, confused and restless. They rallied around the child because of his strength and his light. He welcomed them and guided them. They loved him unconditionally and he returned that love. He had a job to do. They gathered around him and listened for directions. He had a plan, and with his plan, he would achieve retribution. This would be his final move, the one he had been waiting for, the one he had been born to make.

Chapter Nineteen
Harmon Springs
1957

He was born
To protect you,
No one will understand.
We all will misunderstand
His love

"Hey, sweetie, what are you up to?" Clarisse walked into Annabelle's room and saw that she was concentrating hard on a little slip of paper.

"I'm writing a poem," Annabelle answered without looking up.

Clarisse sat carefully at the edge of her daughter's bed. Annabelle didn't like to be touched or moved or disturbed. "Oh? What is it about?" she craned to look at the slip of paper.

"It's about a girl who sees ghosts." Annabelle willingly handed the poem to her mother.

The girl sat quietly
Eyes down, waiting
Waiting for the ghost -
The boy to release her
And to forgive those
Who needed forgiveness.

"What a strange poem Annabelle. Why does she need forgiveness?"

"She doesn't mom. The boy does. And he needs to forgive others but he can't because he doesn't know how. He needs her to show him."

"Oh, Annabelle, you are so creative." She handed the poem back to her twelve-year-old daughter. Annabelle was still looking down, concentrating on a new slip of paper. "Do you have your math lessons done for the day?"

"Yes ma'am. They are on my desk."

Clarisse stood up, her joints aching and walked over to the desk to examine the lessons. They were perfect, as usual. She couldn't figure it out. Annabelle was brilliant, creative, thoughtful, and quiet; all the qualities anyone would want in a child. But she couldn't be touched or jostled. She couldn't function in a group of people. She complained of voices, both loud and quiet, in her ears. She snuck out and walked in the predawn hours until the sun was rising.

She needed outlets for her creativity. Annabelle's poetry was haunting and beautiful. Clarisse desperately wanted her daughter to fit Ken's definition of "normal" so that he would embrace her and love her. But, she looked over at Annabelle, lying on her bed, concentrating on her poems. Her daughter personified brilliance at work and she, her mother, was the only one who knew.

Chapter Twenty
Harmon Springs
2000

A doctor's hand
Heals
And destroys,
The good, the bad
His hands search the dark,
Feeling for life
Only finding
His corrupted flesh.

"Peter, you're not making sense. Why do you think the sheriff at Harmon Springs wants to hurt us?" Angie kept her eyes on the road, watching for the exit.

Peter, sweating with pain, grunted. "I told you, there is a link between Iron Rope and Harmon Springs. I tried to find you at Harmon Springs and they were just, I don't know, weird."

"Weird. That is the best you can describe it? They had better have a hospital. Jesus. This is crazy." She took the exit and headed back to a place that she did not remember, but a place that remembered her completely. She looked over at Peter, who was in a shock – like sleep. She was reminded of what children do in times of extreme stress. They sleep.

The scenery changed from farmland to scattered homes, then to some weather-worn gas stations and small, well-used farm buildings. Then the faded and beaten sign loomed, crooked, proclaiming, "Welcome to Harmon Springs pop 48,000." Hello people. I'm home, Angie whispered to herself.

A population of 1,009 should hopefully warrant some sort of medical facility. Angie followed a sign promising just such a place. She pulled up to a tiny building that seemed too small to be any help. Its emergency doors were the only ones with lights on. She parked and whispered to Peter, who could not hear her, "I'm going to go get help. I'll be right back. Don't move." She fumbled out of the car, locked the doors, a habit of city living, and raced into the building.

"Hello ma'am, how can I help you?" The nurse at the admitting desk eyed her curiously.

"My friend is hurt. He's out in my car and he's unconscious."

The nurse handed her some forms, "Okay, ma'am, can you fill these out and let us know which car is yours?"

"Really?" She shoved the papers back at the secretary, "I can't fill these out right now, and there are no other cars out there but mine...you can't miss it. It has an unconscious man in it."

"Ma'am, we need you to calm down. We have procedures here. We are going to help your friend. We just need some information." The nurse called someone while Angie grudgingly took the paperwork. She was filling out the forms when a doctor cleared his throat to get her attention.

"Hello, Miss. I'm Doctor Shaun Ray. I think you came in with a young man unconscious in your car?"

"Um. Yes, he fell and broke his arm. He is in my car and ..."

"Yes, miss, can you take me to your car?" He held out his hand to gather the paperwork from her. He took a quick glance at the top form and looked up at her, "Yes, Miss Simpson, let's go take a look."

"Finally. Okay, right this way." They walked out to her car. There was something wrong.

"Is this your car Miss Simpson?" He motioned to her car, sympathetically.

She was confused. "Yes, but he must have gotten out. I told him to stay put. Maybe someone came and got him out already..." she unlocked the passenger car door. The seat was filled with her overnight bag, odd fast food bags, and many maps in different stages of folding nightmares. No Peter. The doctor folded his arms and looked concerned. "No, wait. He was here. I don't know why this stuff is here. He fell, he fell out of the window..." she stood shaking her head.

The doctor put his hand on her shoulder. "Miss Simpson, have you been traveling long? I think I might suggest getting a room and getting some sleep." He kindly guided her back around to the driver's side of her car.

"I don't understand. Where did he go? I have to find him. Are you sure he didn't go inside?" She turned to go back inside, and the doctor stopped her.

"No, ma'am, he didn't go inside. We do not have any new patients. There is a motel a mile down the road, on the right. Get some rest before you drive anymore. Doctor's orders." He opened her car door and guided her into the driver's seat. She willingly sat in the driver's seat, though unable to look at the filled passenger seat. Before he closed the door, he repeated, "Get some rest, Miss Simpson. Please, before you travel anymore."

She rolled up her window to keep out the dampness of the humidity. She had read about the humidity that sat heavily in river valleys. The stories were not exaggerations. As she started the car, she glanced sideways at the passenger seat. It was full of her things. She started the car because she didn't know what else to do. She was not leaving this town without him. Something happened; someone took him for whatever reason. She was going to find him. Then she was going to find out about her mother and then she was getting the hell out of here.

The motel was down the street as promised. A sleepy clerk gave her the key to her room. She left her overnight bag in the seat, unwilling to believe that it was even really there. She opened the door to her room and sat on the bed, which creaked. She was tired. Confused. Angry.

When she woke in the morning, she didn't remember lying down, much less falling asleep. Her dreams were glimpses of Peter falling from an empty window, doctors smiling sympathetically at her, exit signs and welcome signs. She woke with a start as a ray of sunshine pierced the gap in the curtains.

She stepped out to look at her car again. She walked cautiously over to the passenger side and peered through the window. The seat was the same as last night: filled with her things. She walked over to the office of the motel. The sleepy clerk was replaced with a bright-faced young man who perked up noticeably as she approached him.

"Hi, I was wondering if you could help me out with some directions?" She hoped she didn't sound as crazy as she felt.

"Oh, sure! You ain't from 'round here. Whatcha lookin' for?"

"I need to find the police department," she noted the quizzical look on his face, "or the sheriff?"

"Oh, yeah, sheriff's office is downtown, on the square." He smiled at her but she didn't respond. "Oh, um, right down this street and then take a left and you will be downtown. You can't miss it."

"Thank you."

"Hey, no problem. Do you need the room for another night?" There was more than hope in his voice. She considered him for two seconds; he was all of maybe eighteen. Flattered but a bit nauseated at the same time, she shook her head.

"No, here's the key. I just have something to finish really quick and I'm on my way." He was visibly let down.

"Well, it was nice meetin' ya. Let me know if you need anythin' okay?"

"I will, thanks." She walked away, feeling his eyes pressed hard on her butt. She tried to walk with an extra shake for him; it was the least she could do. She remembered that Peter had visited the sheriff; he may have found his way back there. So the sheriff's office first, then back to that "hospital" or clinic or whatever they considered it. He was too injured to have gone far.

Angie opened her car door, and she wondered if the doors were locked when she took the doctor out to show him where Peter was passed out. She couldn't remember. She backed out of the parking space and kept glancing uneasily at the passenger seat as she searched for downtown Harmon Springs. She saw the edge of a small card sticking out of the pile of her things. She grabbed it. It was a business card - a business card from the director at Iron Rope. Peter had to have been there – right there in her car.

Angie drove slowly, which was good since the speed limit was 15 mph. She twirled the card as she appraised the town. The town was quaint, quiet and tiny. It seemed that the acceptable form of transportation was the golf cart. She felt out of place with all her horsepower. She found the city square easily enough. She parked, put money in an ancient meter, and slid the card into her back pocket.

The sheriff's station was a perfect replica of a Norman Rockwell drawing. She pushed open the wooden and glass pained door. There was no one at the front counter. She looked around for a bell. No luck.

"Hello! Excuse me! Anybody home?" she guessed the crime rate in this place was probably not very high. A heavy-set older woman entered from some back room.

"Oh, hello there, ma'am. How can I help you? I am so sorry for your wait."

"Hi, I'm looking for someone. He actually was here a day ago, actually asking for me, ironically enough." She sounded crazy.

The lady cocked her head. "You say he came here looking for you and now you are looking for him? Is that right?"

"Yes, his name is Peter, Peter…"

"I'm so sorry, ma'am. We haven't seen any strangers in quite some time. I would know, I'm the only secretary here, and there ain't been no visitors in a long while." She smiled sweetly at Angie.

"Well, that's odd. I could swear he said he stopped in here." She steadied herself on the counter. He had said that in the car. Maybe he wasn't really ever in the car, which would make sense if he was never here, either, right? Her thoughts were racing faster than her heart.

"Ma'am, are you okay? Lemme get you some water, you look pale." The secretary fumbled in another room getting a drink. Angie took the moment to look at what the secretary was working on. There were plans of the Iron Rope Sanatorium spread out on her desk with notes and pencil marks in seemingly strategic places. She also noticed marks all over the grounds. The marks were in orderly rows, circling the building. The secretary stepped back into the room, holding the water in a paper cup. She looked at Angie and then down at the plans.

"Is that the sanatorium, um, Iron Rope Sanatorium?" Angie asked innocently. She knew she had been caught. The secretary handed her the water roughly.

"Why, yes it is. The Sheriff is planning on remodeling it," the now agitated secretary replied as she shuffled the blueprints into a manila folder. "I'm sorry, I can't help you." She turned, effectively dismissing her.

Angie had a crazy idea. "Is he here, the Sheriff?"

The secretary did not look up but busied herself with other documents on the desk. "No, he's not here right now, ma'am. You might wanna try back later. He ain't made it in yet today."

"Okay, thank you." She hoped it sounded as snarky as she wanted it to. This definitely must be a low crime town. The sheriff didn't even have to report on time for work? She left the office and surveyed the street. People were walking about and driving around in golf carts. She watched them as they stopped to greet each other and catch up on local gossip. The shops were warm and inviting. Harmon Springs had everything from antiques to homemade soaps to an old-time opera house. She was getting nowhere fast.

One little business caught her eye. "Annabelle's Cafe." From the windows, Angie could see it was a small, deli-type eatery. A coincidence? She knew she needed to find Peter, but she was drawn to the little restaurant and walked towards it in a dream-like state.

She crossed the street and entered the small establishment. A bell rang as she opened the door. There was a bar area, and a young waitress taking care of regulars. The smell of hot coffee and cinnamon scones surrounded her. She grabbed a table near the back of the odd, rectangular-shaped dining room. She tried to push her restaurant 'take everything apart skills' aside as she looked up at the menu written on the chalkboard. That was promising; maybe only local fresh ingredients necessitated a more changeable menu listing. A young waitress came over to her table.

"Hi, have you had a chance to decide what you want for breakfast?" She didn't have any type of order slip. That always bothered Angie, but she was trying to be good.

"Yes, I would like a strawberry scone and a coffee."

"Cream or no?"

"Yes, some cream would be nice."

"Okay, will do." She quickly returned with the order.

"Anything else?"

"Kind of. Do you have a history of this place, like something that tells how it started?"

The waitress's eyes lit up. "I knew it! You're from one of those food channels, aren't you?"

"Oh no, sorry to disappoint. I'm just curious about the name of the place." Angie smiled sweetly, trying to smooth over the girl's now hurt face.

"It's named after the owner's daughter. It's kind of a long story and I would like to help you, but my regulars are comin' in. But I bet Redd will talk to ya. He is sittin' there at the end of the bar. He loves

talkin' history and 'tales of long ago.' He misses talkin' about the
history of our town. We used to get lots more tourists, but since they
built that highway, well, people just don't come through here." She
left to go wait on her regulars.

Angie picked up her coffee and scone and made her way to the
end of the counter. Redd was eating his way through eggs and toast.
The waitress appeared again behind the counter. "Hey Redd, this
nice lady is needn' some information. You think you could oblige
her? There's a free slice of rhubarb pie in it for ya."

Redd grunted but smiled at her. "Now Betty Lou, you know you
don't have to go and do that. But since you offered, I guess I could
help out." He swiveled in his chair and held out his hand in greeting.
"Hi, I'm Redd."

Angie took his hand. It was large, warm, and calloused. At first,
she thought he was older, in his eighties, but then after he spoke, she
wasn't sure. He had an agelessness about him.

"I'm Angie. So nice to meet you." She tried not to sound like she
was in a hurry. She wanted to fit the casual atmosphere. "I just
wanted to ask you a couple of questions. The nice young lady said
you were a wealth of knowledge about the history of this town." It
was natural for her to lay on the charm first. It was a habit and a skill
she learned from working with so many disgruntled restaurant
owners and workers.

He chuckled, "Well, I don't know about that, but I do know some
things. What do you want to hear about?"

"For starters, the name of this place. She said it was named after
the owner's daughter. Can you fill me in on that story?"

"Yeah, that's an easy one. Years ago, our mayor at the time,
Kenneth Mason, met an untimely end. He died in an automobile
accident down in the bottoms. It was dark that night; foggy, too. He
ran right off the road and hit a tree. So sad. The missus was much
loved in the town. God bless her heart. She was a teacher, but after
her husband passed, she closed up her books and opened up this here
eatery. She named it after her only daughter. Now Annabelle, their
daughter- that is a story worth tellin'. How much time you got?"

"Not much, but I'm listening."

"Well, Annabelle was touched you, know." He pointed to his
head. "She killed one of her newborn twins, and she was committed
for it. The other one was adopted out. No one knows what happened

to her. The family moved out of town when the mill closed. Mrs. Mason was a broken woman. I know'd that she felt bad for never taking care of her grandchild and losin' her own child to a sanatorium. We used to talk about it for hours. Well, she built this place in honor of her daughter. God rest both their souls. Mrs. Mason passed this spring. So sad, but she did pass in her sleep, so she felt no pain or nothin'." He pulled his beard thoughtfully and his rheumy eyes focused on something outside the paned window.

"I am so sorry to hear that." Angie slowly stirred her coffee. That would have been her grandmother. She missed her by months. A sadness began to sit on her heart. "So, she was active in running this place until she passed?"

"Oh, hell yes, pardon my French. She was healthy, mentally and physically. The doctors couldn't explain why she died. They just said it was her time to go. I think she was just plain sad and it finally took over her heart."

"Sad because of her husband and daughter?"

"Well, maybe, but, mostly she was sad about Annabelle's baby girl. She didn't want to adopt her out, but her husband wanted no part of raising that baby. Then he up and died a year after it all happened. Clarisse, that's Mrs. Mason's first name, she tried to find the family, but they left with no forwarding address. They was strange folk, them Simpsons. They had kinfolk here too, but they never contacted anyone. It's like they was runnin' from somethin'.

"After all that mess, so much happened to this town. The mill closin' was hard on people. Whole families moved out trying to keep their families fed. So sad." The waitress filled his cup. "Betty Lou, you remember how Mrs. Mason used to talk about the good ole days, when this town was alive? She was such a great lady. Sad, but she was great at helpin' people. Why, there were times when she knew you couldn't pay for food, and she would take you up on your word and you could pay on credit. Ain't that right?"

"Yes. She was a nice boss. I do miss her." The waitress smiled a smile that was full of sweet memories of a good lady who was gone.

"She sounds amazing. Thank you for your time. I do really appreciate it. I have to get moving though. My friend is missing, and I need to find him. He's hurt and probably delirious somewhere." She laid a $20 on the counter.

"Oh, really? What's his name? I'm so sorry; you probably need to get moving for sure." Redd perked up. Angie could see an instant change from a man lost in sad memory to a man who could be of purpose today.

"His name is Peter. He has short, black hair, stands about 6 foot, on a good day," she smiled, thinking how proud he was of his new loafers with a bit of a heal, "and he has kind of feminine features. The most telling thing is that his arm is badly broken. "

"His arm is broken and you don't know where he is?" Redd's curiosity was apparent.

"It's such a long story, and I promise I will come back and share so much of it with you guys, you probably will beg me to shut up. I've got to go though."

"Well, okay miss. If you need help, you just stop back by. Our sheriff is super helpful too, if it looks like you need help in that area." She could tell from the look in his eyes that he was genuinely worried about the situation. Besides Peter, she couldn't remember anyone being genuinely worried about her. Most people were like the secretary at the police station.

Yeah, I've already been there. She replied, "Oh, thank you. Have a great day." She walked out as calmly as possible. There was so much she wanted to tell them, but there just wasn't time. Her grandmother was loved and respected. There was something strange about her grandfather, something unsaid, but they did exist. My grandmother wanted me.

Now her first stop was that medical clinic, then back to Iron Rope. Peter had to be in one of those places.

The clinic turned up nothing but concerned vacant stares. She figured as much. She put the car in drive after filling up at a gas station that insisted on pumping the gas for her. It was odd, and she wasn't sure what to do with herself, stay in the car? Stand outside? By the time she decided she should step out of the car, he was at the window to collect the money. She smiled up at him, handed him the cash.

"Thank you miss. You have a great day, now ya' hear?" He winked and stepped away from her car.

She rolled up her window, nodding at him and smiling and muttering through her teeth, "Yes, I'm not in Kansas anymore." Creepy factor number 109, she thought to herself. Of course, what could be creepier than visiting an abandoned lunatic asylum looking for a lost friend? She dug out her cigarettes with one hand as she pulled onto the highway. She checked her phone for any sign of life. No service.

She continued the hour and a half drive back to the abandoned building. There were a few differences driving the route in the daytime hours. One thing that was not different was that the drive was quiet; once again, she didn't pass one car. She did note a few well-tended homesteads. She rode by them quickly, but a blank spot in the landscape caught her eye. It was a cemetery. She made a mental note to come back and explore that. Her family could be buried there unless they had a private plot on some land somewhere.

The ailing institution loomed in the distance. A cold, creeping feeling started inching its way up her spine. She pulled up in the same space she had left, next to Peter's car.

When she stepped out of her car, she immediately covered her nose. Something was dead. An animal, a very large animal was decaying somewhere. She glanced uncertainly around her. She walked over to Peter's car. It was locked. Nothing was bothered. I know he wouldn't go anywhere without his car, she thought. She looked up at the window he jumped from and paced over to the place where he would have fallen. She was no bounty hunter but the ground did not look like a man of 140 pounds fell there. Was he really in my car? Did we even really have that conversation? Maybe she was having a blackout then, or maybe now. What is real? She remembered the business card and retrieved it from her back pocket. He had to have been in her car. How else would this card have gotten there?

She walked to the front doors. They were sealed solidly, but this time she could feel a cool breeze coming from between the old boards that were meant to keep people out. She pushed. The dry rotted wood fell apart enough for her to see inside. She peeked her head in feeling like she should quote that line from *The Shining* but thought better of it.

It was dark inside, yet there was a breeze coming through. There was another opening somewhere; however, she had explored all around the building before and hadn't seen any other opening. She must have missed something. She pulled the rest of the boards apart, gathering her fair share of splinters. The opening was large enough to squeeze through.

"Peter! Can you hear me?" The echo of her voice answered over and over. She pulled her phone from her pocket, still no service.

She took a big breath and crawled through the opening. She felt carefully for the floor on the other side. Hadn't he said that there was a huge sinkhole right at the front entrance? The floor seemed solid.

She stood up and gave her eyes a moment to adjust. The front hall must have been very impressive in its time. The ceilings were high, twenty or more feet; the walls looked like they may have once been decorated with ornate bas-reliefs of cherubs. Now they were crumbling and covered with mold. Water was dripping somewhere. The dead smell hadn't followed her in here, luckily, but the mildew assaulted her nose just as harshly.

A long hallway was directly in front of her. Each side also had long hallways. I'm following the breeze. It's probably what he would have done. He hates weird smells. The breeze would have been refreshing.

She took a tentative step and her foot landed in a puddle of water. Why was it so wet in here? She also noted that there was no gaping pit in front of the door, or anywhere to be seen. She headed forward, down the main hallway. "Peter?" She whispered. Only dripping water answered.

As she walked down the hallway, she glanced inside rooms with rotted-out doors. There were remnants of bed frames piled in broken pieces. Rats scurried as she disturbed their infested slumbers. She was painfully aware that she needed a flashlight. She walked past some desk-like area that must have been a nurse's station. She took a peek behind the partition. Cabinets were hanging, doors long gone. Broken chairs lay around as if some crazy tornado cruised through what was probably a very neat and orderly nurse's station. She stepped back and saw her handprints in the dust on the counter. No one had been in here for a very long time. He didn't come this way for sure.

The rest of the hallway was dark, but she could see some light further down, natural light streaming in, maybe where the breeze was coming from. She continued on. Rooms, open and exposed, sat quietly as she walked down the hallway.

A closed room caught her attention. She touched the doorknob; it was slimy but gave way to a dark room. She swung the door wide trying to see if the hallway light could help her see what was inside. "Peter?" she whispered into the room. Why am I whispering? Really, like is someone sleeping? "Peter!" She yelled. No echo. She could make out that the room was made up of rows and rows of shelves. Maybe a linen closet? She shrugged and closed the door.

"Peter!" she yelled down the hallway again. Something fell. A distinct falling sound, like how a body might sound if it was falling over. "Peter, is that you? Can you hear me?" she rushed on. So many rooms. The way was more visible as she reached the lighted area. It was a big broken window. She stepped up to it and saw that it looked out onto a walled-in courtyard. It looked like it could have been beautiful at one time. She leaned forward a bit to gulp the fresh air. "Peter! Can you hear me?"

A scuffling noise whirled her around. She followed the sound. There was another closed door where the hallway turned. She turned the knob and it opened easily. The room was an office of some type. There was another floor to ceiling window. The room would have been posh if it hadn't been covered in mildew and slime. "Peter, are you in here?" the scuffling noise brought her attention to another door in the room.

She opened the door and there on the floor gagged and bound was her friend Peter. "Oh my God, Peter!" She grabbed him up, he staggered and blinked his eyes in the sunlight. "What the hell happened to you?" She took the gag out of his mouth and turned him around to untie his hands and feet. She rested her hand on his arm. "Oh, I'm sorry; did I hurt your arm?"

"My arm? No. What the hell is going on? Why did you leave me? The patients jumped me and tied me up!" He shook his head and steadied himself.

"I didn't leave you! What are you talking about? I came...."

"No. You told me we were dead and that I had to accept that. Then the doctor said that we had to stay and..."

Angie put her hands on the sides of Peter's head to make him focus on her. "Peter, is there someone else in here with us? I think someone is screwing with us. Listen to me. We are leaving right now."

Peter was looking past her at the area where a large desk used to sit. "No, Angie, I don't think we are leaving."

"Oh, yes we are. Come on."

"No," Peter held out his arm to stop her, "I don't think he is going to let us." Angie turned, slowing to look at what stopped Peter. There sitting in the corner of the room, was a young child. He was quietly watching them.

"A kid? In here?" She took a step towards the child. "Hey there, little guy. Do you need some help? What are you doing here?" With each step, the child stiffened. She stopped.

"Angie, don't do it. I don't think he - "

Angie waved him to be quiet. "Hey, don't be scared. I'm Angie and this is my friend Peter. We just want to get out of here. Do you need some help finding your way out? Are there any adults here with you?" She inched closer.

The child looked amused. He giggled and covered his mouth.

"Okay creepy little kid, we are just going to leave you here. God, I hate kids." She backed away from the giggling child and backed up towards the door. "Let's go, Peter. Follow me."

They ran through the door and down the hall. She stopped them at the disheveled nurses' station, out of breath.

"I really should quit smoking. Do you think he is following us?" She leaned over, trying to breathe.

"No," Peter replied, "but I don't think he is who we need to worry about."

"What do you mean?" she huffed.

"There is a doctor here. He's who we need to worry about."

"A doctor? I don't know what is creepier, a random creepy kid or a creepy doctor. We are outta here." She grabbed her side and his hand, and they ran down the hallway.

"Hey, wait," he gasped, "this room here, one second."

"No, Peter, come on. There's nothing in there."

"Yes, wait; it's the records room. We need to go in there super-fast. Your mom's things are in there."

"Really?" she hesitated. She looked down the hall; she could just make out the main entryway. "Are you sure?"

"Yes, come on. I know where they are."

"How?" But he was already in the room. "Where did you go? It is so dark in here. Peter?" she felt along the wall instinctively looking for a light.

"Ouch! Hold on a sec. I know where it is. Just stay right there."

"Peter, I hear giggling. Come on. We can come back with a team of people; this stuff isn't going anywhere. That kid is coming." She peeked out into the hallway but didn't see anything.

"I got it." He was carrying a cardboard box. "Okay, let's go. Wait. There is one more thing." He dropped the box at her feet and went back into the darkness.

"Peter, come on." She reached down to open the box. It was full of papers. The ones on top looked like some type of drawings. She picked one up and looked at a baby picture of her. "These are of me...are these hers?" Her voice sounded small in the darkness. "Peter?" she looked up trying to see into the black. "Peter! Answer me!" The giggling was louder now. She stood up and put her back against the damp wall. The giggling stopped right outside the door. "Peter," she whispered. "Stay where you are."

"I am." His voice was next to her ear. She jumped.

"God, Peter, let's go."

Peter moved to block the door. "No, we can't go yet. You have to hear what he has to say."

"What? Who? Creepy kid? Um. No, we're leaving. Let's go. Move out of the way." She tried to move, but he stopped her. She wondered fleetingly about his broken arm, but it didn't seem to be hurt now. The giggling started up again.

"Peter, you're scaring me. Please, let's go." Peter looked at her, holding her by the shoulders.

"We can go, but first you have to listen to him. You have to trust me. It's the only way. You trust me, don't you?" Trust wasn't her strong point, but she did trust him. Peter stepped aside and the child skipped in and sat on the box. Peter moved back to block the door. She looked at him and then back at the child.

"Okay, I'm listening. You don't have to hit me with a cosmic two by four." Peter seemed to relax. She was thinking how hard it would be to push him aside and make a run for it. But could she leave him here with the giggler?

"Angela. You are so much prettier than I thought you would be." The voice came from the child, she knew it came from the child, but the child's mouth did not move. It was an adult voice that spoke. The child just sat there smiling crazily at her and Peter. She started to back up towards the door.

"No, Angela, I'm sorry. You can't leave right now." Every time he spoke, the lights flickered and the walls changed from moldy to clean. "It's okay, don't be afraid. I just want to talk to you." She watched the lights flicker longer and then stay on. They were in a records room. The shelves were lined with boxes that seemed to go on forever. "This is what it looked like years ago. Much better, don't you think?" The voice seemed amused at itself. Angie glanced over at Peter. He was looking down and there was a large bump and gash on the side of his head that she had not noticed before.

"Oh, he is fine, don't worry, I wouldn't let anything happen to him. That would take away the fun. We like fun."

"What's going on? Look. I don't believe in ghosts, and if this is a crazy prank or something, then you win, okay? Now can we go?"

"No, Angela. Not yet. Come sit here beside me. You, too, Peter." The child gestured to the floor by the box. Peter moved as if on autopilot. He sat at first on his knees.

"No! Not like that! Indian style, criss-cross apple sauce!" The disembodied voice yelled. Peter adjusted and crossed his legs. Angie followed suit, crossing her legs but angling her body so she could see the door.

"That is so funny that you think you are going to run out of here. Why are you always trying to leave me? Are you ready for storytime?"

Peter nodded though it was hard to tell because he was still looking at the floor.

"Angela?"

"Yes," she sighed.

"Good!" the voice was pleased, and the child clapped his hands. The child then pretended to open a book. "Angela, I'm so glad you are here. I have been waiting a long time to read you a story. Are you comfortable?"

This is crazy. She nodded, trying to figure out where the voice was coming from.

"Good. Stop worrying and listen to my story. Okay, let's begin." The child's body moved to cross its ankles and began to read from some invisible book.

"Once upon a time there was a beautiful maiden. She was coveted by anyone who met her. This was because she was so incredibly beautiful, not just on the outside, but on the inside also. She had raven black hair and big, dark, mysterious eyes. She captivated both men and women when she walked through town." The voice paused dramatically. Angie looked over at Peter and saw that he was crying quietly.

"Peter…why are you…?"

"Shhhhhh! I'm telling a story. Don't interrupt! Don't worry about him; he has already heard this part. Now just listen."

She sighed and assumed the same position as Peter. The story continued.

"As I was saying, the woman was beautiful. It just so happened one night that she had some visitors to her manor. They had promised her beautiful gifts for her generosity of spirit. She was pleased to be recognized for her efforts for helping others. They entered her manor, and something very dark happened. They raped her over and over. They held her down and took advantage of her for three days. She was confused and scared for her life. They used her in every way possible and laughed at her when they finally got their fill. They left her eventually, bloody and swollen and ugly on the floor of her great front room. She cried and prayed for revenge for retribution for this horrendous crime. Her prayers were answered and she became pregnant with twins. She was promised retribution for the crimes committed against her through the birth of her children.

"One of the men returned ten months after the crime to claim one of the children. He was unaware that there were two children born to her. She willingly gave her child to the man. This gift would start the cycle of redemption. This child was our mother, Annabelle." The child clapped his hands again at the surprise on Angie's face.

"Annabelle grew up in a small town not far from her real mother's home. The family that raised her was a flawed family, but it was the perfect family because of the promised redemption. The adopted father was one of the criminals that raped our mother, and it was a perfect night when he raped his adopted daughter, his true daughter, and produced us. Unfortunately, I was a weak baby. I tried to protect you but the other criminal came in one day and smothered me. I understood that I was just part of the plan, but I was saddened that there would be no one to watch over you. Once I lost my earthly form, I found that it was much easier to help the plan along. Some things, unfortunately, were out of my control. I thought that they would murder you too because that was their plan, but we all know what happens with best-laid plans. You lived. I died. So, I spent all of this time gaining retribution for our mother, our grandmother, and myself. Do you want to guess how our story ends?"

Angie looked at the child who now looked wan and tired. She didn't answer; she didn't know how to respond. Silence surrounded them. "You are my brother?" she addressed the child who was no longer smiling. He had deep, dark, impossibly dark circles under his eyes. She strained to see any resemblance. "Jacob?" At the utterance of the name, the child crawled off the box and went to sit against the far wall.

"No, Angela, that isn't Jacob, I'm Jacob, but you can't understand me as I am, so I am using this child to help you better comprehend what I'm trying to tell you. I have hurt many people. I have protected you, and now I'm ready to end the cycle. I need you to help me."

"Did you kill our mother?"

"No. Sister. He killed her. An evil man killed her. He was addicted to a drug, and out of his mind. He hated her because she knew his weakness. Our mother was evidence of his malpractice. I tried to help her, but it was too hard. It is difficult to influence the world of the living when the world of the living is strong. But when a person is weak, that is when I can gain control. He was weak. I was able to make him pay for her death. He paid with his life."

Angie asked, whispering, "How many people have you killed, Jacob?"

"Many."

"Are you going to kill us?"

"I wasn't born to kill you. I was born to protect you from the curse. The debt is paid, but the hate still lingers."

She lifted her head, trying to shake a fog out of it. "Jacob. If this is really you, and you really are trying to protect me or whatever, then you have to know I'm scared. You have to know that my friend is hurt. If you love me, then you have to let me go. Let us go."

The voice hummed around her. "I need you. I'm so tired. And I have one last thing I need to accomplish. But before that, you have to know what happened to the criminals. The final retribution is letting the world know the truth."

"I don't care really, it doesn't have anything to do with me, and my friend is hurt..."

The voice roared, "Yes, it does! It has everything to do with you. Your father is also your grandfather. The criminal that killed me wanted to kill you. This is important. I killed our adopted grandmother, but not out of madness; I killed her to put her out of her misery. She really did love you Angela. Her heart was broken when they sent you away, but it had already been breaking because deep down she knew her husband was our father. Luckily, she never knew that Annabelle was his daughter. That would have broken her further. I killed her to set her free."

"Okay, so you are like some sort of avenger, vigilante, and now you are done. So what could be left?"

"That is up to you."

She glanced over at the motionless child, eyes open, dead along the wall. "What did that kid do? Was he a criminal?"

"He isn't real, Angela. He died years ago here at the asylum. I animated him to help speak to you. I animated Peter to help you see the events unfolding in Harmon Springs as I also animated you to keep Peter here, safe with me. I animated the doctor to help Peter see that I am serious about what must happen next.

"Did you know that the sheriff's son is planning on tearing down this building?" The voice mourned the next words, "these are my people, and these lost souls, where will we go if this place no longer exists? I have taken care of most of the lost and angry souls in here. They all come to me to help guide them, and they help me in return. However, am weary of fighting, weary of protecting, but I have a job to do. Sister. I am asking for your help."

Angie reached over and touched Peter's knee. He didn't look up, but he wasn't crying anymore.

"Do you ever wonder, dear sister, at your relationship with Peter? Do you wonder at how at times, you finish each other's sentences? Do you wonder why you can trust no one, but you can trust him?" Now it was Angie's turn to cry. "Yes, you know that he is related to you. Twins run in our family, you know. Our grandmother, Janelle, kept one twin. That girl child grew and delivered a child and that child is Peter. He is your cousin. So see, you do have family."

Angie wiped her eyes and looked over at the child. He was a rotting skeleton now. "What do you want?"

"I have spent all these years helping souls and delivering justice. Now I just want one last bit of justice. I want you to go to my earthly body and show the world what happened to me. I want you to vindicate our mother's name. I want a proper burial, here on these grounds, next to the unmarked grave where our mother is buried. I can help you, but you must perform the actions. I am tired, Angela. I'm ready to join our mother. Before this place is torn down, the bodies must be identified and buried properly. I have a duty to these souls."

"And if I don't help, then what? You will kill us? Haunt us forever? What?"

"I think you will help me, but if you do not, then I will continue to do what I'm doing now. But I hope that you will help me if only to help Peter who seems to need medical attention."

She noted that Peter was pale and unmoving but still upright. "You are controlling him, aren't you?"

"Yes."

"But, he is alive, not dead like the child," she looked over at the pile of dust and rags where the child was.

"Yes, he is alive, for now."

"And are you controlling me? Am I alive?"

"No. I am not controlling you. I have protected you. Now you are safe. Now I am asking for something in return."

"But I didn't ask to be protected. Why do I have to -?"

"Please," Jacob's voice waivered.

"Why did you have to scare us? Why couldn't you just tell me? I don't understand."

"I was angry, so very angry. I had been planning this vindication, this retribution, and I was ready for vengeance. Then, once you were really here, I couldn't do it anymore. I watched you and I knew I could never hurt you. I was going to, and I was going to hurt everyone you loved. Then I realized my role was to protect you just for this reason. The hate, the curse set forth by our grandmother, took on a life of its own." Angie looked over at Peter who was still dazed. "Yes, I was going to kill him. I was so jealous that they all got to love you; they all got to be a part of your life. But I, who loved you more than anyone, didn't even get a chance to be in your life. But look at you. You are strong. You are brave. You are beautiful. I am humbled, and now I am tired. Please help me, sister. Please." A small dark shadow manifested in front of her. She reached out to touch him. "No, you can't touch what isn't there, sister. Please help me."

Chapter Twenty One
Harmon Springs
2000

It takes love
To heal the hate
He was born to love
No one understood
Her curse became
Its own energy
Which cannot be
Created
Or destroyed

When she pulled up to the clinic, for the third time, she sighed. "Peter, I know you are hurt, and weak, but you have to come in with me, I'm not leaving you out here again."

He looked over at her, "Again?"

"It's another long story. Come on, let's get you some help."

"Well, I don't want to sit through another story time, that's for sure," he grumbled as he unlatched his seatbelt. "I feel like I've been in a dream. Was all of that real? Angie, are you real?"

"Yes, I'm real. I think it was all real. I can't get my head around it. Let's get you some help." Angie helped Peter into the clinic. The admitting nurse skipped the step of the filling out of papers as she noted Peter's battered head. The nurse helped Angie get him on a stretcher. "This is Peter. He is my friend, and he is hurt," as the words tumbled out of her, she cried. The nurse patted Angie's back and then took Peter to a room for x-rays and stitches. Angie watched him being wheeled away. My friend. My cousin. The words sat heavily in her heart.

Angie needed to work quickly. "Ma'am? Can you tell Peter I'll be right back? I need to check on something in town."

The receptionist, the same one who hassled her on her first visit, nodded and continued reading a book.

As she walked out of the clinic, Angie pulled her hastily sketched map of the local cemetery, based on Jacob's descriptions, and with it was a charcoal drawn picture of her. Her mother's art. She didn't

realize she had kept it. She carried it back to her car and slid it inside
a spiral she had in her backseat. She shut her car door and headed to
Annabelle's Cafe to talk to Redd.

The bells sent a faint song as she opened the door to the café. The
same waitress was busily cleaning the well-used coffee pot. She
turned automatically at the sound of the bells and recognized her
customer. "Hi, did you find your friend?"

"I did, thanks. Have you seen Redd?"

"I think he went to see his granddaughter. I doubt he will be back
today. Can I help you with something?"

"No, I'm good. Thanks." Angie left Annabelle's Café and walked
out into the warm country air. She pondered as she looked around at
the sleepy town. How am I going to do this? I need to get permission
to exhume a grave to reveal a murder. Then I have to convince
everyone that the murder was not committed by my mother, but by
the old sheriff. Then the business with the asylum itself. Maybe I
should just let it alone. She noticed that she was walking back to her
car. Going back to the clinic. Yes, Peter will know what to do. It
wasn't like her not to know. She was always a leader, a take-charge
kind of person. Now she couldn't even decide where to go or how to
go about doing what needed to get done.

The admitting nurse at the clinic smiled reassuringly. "Hello,
Miss Simpson. Your friend is doing fine. Would you like me to take
you to see him?"

"Yes, that will be nice." Angie let the nurse lead her to Peter's
room. The clinic was clean, small, and she could see that the staff
was caring and concerned about the people of their town. The walls
were covered with memorabilia of Harmon Springs. It did seem odd,
almost museum-like. She passed by a large framed portrait of a
couple and a young girl, all smiling, arms around each other. The
caption at the bottom read "The Mason's." Her voice squeaked
involuntarily. She looked closer at the man's eyes, at the little girl's
eyes; they reflected her eyes. She covered her mouth to hold in a cry
of an unexpected surge of emotion. In one breath, she was happy to
finally see a picture of her mother, father, and grandparents, yet part
of her was appalled that the story was true. Ugly. Dark. Tears fell
down her face as she looked into the faces of the people who could

have been her family, yet were her family. The nurse walked back to Angie as she realized she wasn't following her.

"They were a nice family. Did you know them?" the nurse inquired.

"No, no, I didn't. I came here looking for something, and I found more than I was looking for."

The nurse smiled sympathetically. "Yes, that tends to happen. Life is messy. You can't plan it or expect too much. Peter is right this way."

Angie took one more look at the smiling faces and then followed the nurse.

Peter was sitting up in the bed.

"Well, you look amazing." She plopped on the side of his bed.

"Your sarcasm is refreshing. What the hell happened back there, Angie? Is this real, right now? Was any of that real? I'm really freaked out and I just don't believe it was all because of this head injury." He reached up instinctively to touch the generous bandage wrapped around his head.

"I don't know." Angie adjusted his pillows. "I was just thinking that it was all just some crazy dream. It seems so foggy now. The boy. The story. What exactly do you remember? But I just saw pictures of my, of our family," she watched his reaction to see if he remembered that part.

Peter leaned back, closing his eyes. "He wants us to find his body and vindicate your mother, who was my aunt. Right?" He sat up again, looking at her, "Oh my God, we are family!"

Angie smiled back at him. "I feel like I've known that."

"Me too."

"I don't know how we are going to do what he wants. And don't forget, we have to identify all the bodies in the unmarked graves at Iron Rope and give each one of them a proper burial."

Peter shook his head gingerly. "How are we going to do this, Angie? It seems so impossible. How are we going to get permission to dig up a grave? Maybe we should just forget it and go back home. I think we've found out enough. I don't know about you, but I got bills to pay."

"I don't know. It seems like we are in pretty deep here. If we leave, then supposedly, Jacob will not be at rest. I mean, if all of that was real."

"Angie. When he was 'you,' he said some weird stuff. I don't know what's real."

"What did he say? I mean, when he was me?" she asked, uncertain she wanted to know the answer.

Peter closed his eyes again. "Oh, I dunno. Something about being dead and that we were dead. It was so real. Then that creepy doctor and then it all goes fuzzy." He looked at her, pleading for answers.

"That must be when he took over or whatever, you know, at that fuzzy part?" She ventured.

"Maybe. I remember trying to get out of the building and then nothing."

She pondered aloud. "That must be when 'you' jumped from the window and I brought 'you' here. Why are you laughing?" She smiled at the unexpected sound.

"You know I would never jump out of a window, right? I mean, that sounds very, um…"

"Manly?" she ventured.

"Absolutely."

Angie smiled and added, "But when we were together, hearing the story, that had to be real. How could it not be since we have the same memory?" They both settled into a silence. "I don't know. I met a guy named Redd before I found you. I think he can help us, but I don't know where to find him. He's like the town historian."

There was a knock at the doorframe of the room. "Hello! I'm Dr. Ray. How is my patient feeling today?" He was the same doctor that recommended Angie get some sleep the night before. He began to examine Peter's bandages.

"I'm fine Doc. I probably should be starting the checking out process."

"Well, let's wait just a bit. You have a pretty good gash on that head, 13 staples and a mild concussion. We would like to keep you for a few more hours for observation. Just to be sure." The doctor noted something on a chart that was hanging on Peter's bed. "And how are you doing Miss Simpson?" He asked kindly.

She could not explain it. She could not explain why she felt the urge to tell this man everything that had happened to them. She hesitated because she didn't want him to think she was crazy and have her committed, but she did have Peter to help back up her story. And the closest mental asylum happened to be abandoned. Peter was looking at her, with a look in his eye that told her to give it a try.

"Dr Ray, what do you know about the Iron Rope Sanatorium?"

The Doctor stopped in mid note taking and looked at each of them. "What an odd question. Is that where he received his injuries? That place needs to be torn down. It's dangerous. What do you want to know?" He placed the clipboard back on the end of the bed.

"Well, my mother died there. Her name was Annabelle Mason."

Dr. Ray's face lit up with instant recognition. "You are Annabelle Mason's daughter, Angela?"

She smiled nervously. "You know me?"

"Everyone around here knows your story. Your mother killed your brother and then was committed, and you were adopted out. Yes, I know your story, but I never thought I would ever meet you." His eyes were questioning, but kind.

"I was searching for my mother," Angie adjusted the sheet that covered Peter, "because of some medical issues I had been having." As soon as the words were out of her mouth, she realized - and Peter realized from the way he was looking at her - that she had not had any symptoms of her illness, no blacking out, no voices since this all started.

Dr. Ray, visibly stunned, sat down in the chair next to the bed. "You *are* Angela. How interesting. Did you see their portrait in the hallway?"

"Yes, I did. I hadn't expected to see them face to face. We've been through something. I, I mean, we found out a few very interesting things, and we need someone we can trust to run this information by. Can you help us?"

Dr. Ray hesitated for a moment. "Yes, I want to help you. I failed that family. I want to help you. Let me call in my head nurse to cover the rest of my day."

Peter perked up. "Does this mean I'm discharged?"

The doctor chuckled. "Yes, you'll be with me. I think I can keep an eye on you."

Dr. Ray left the room with a thoughtful smile. Angie looked at Peter. "Is this okay? Do you think he will commit us both?"

"I don't know," Peter answered as he was swinging his legs off the side of the bed, "but I feel like we don't have a choice. I don't know about you, but I don't think I'm willing to go into these good people's cemetery and dig up some beloved relative and find a murdered baby. Sounds kinda crazy."

"Well, when you say it like that. I wonder what he meant about failing the family. He seems to be a kind of historian, just like that guy Redd. The walls are full of portraits of the townspeople and the buildings. I think we need him. We have to trust someone if we want to figure this out."

Peter looked closely at Angie.

"What are you staring at?" Angie asked self-consciously.

"I just want to make sure it's really you. I never thought I would be possessed or tricked or whatever by a ghost. I am going to be a lot more observant from now on."

"Like, about me?"

"About anything. I should have known right away I wasn't dealing with you when you hadn't smoked those cigarettes. I also should have known when you didn't stand up to that crazy doctor. Those should have been big neon signs that you weren't you."

Angie laughed, "And you know what's weird? I don't even want a cigarette. I haven't had one in days. I don't understand it at all. I've smoked since I was like twelve years old. Now the thought of a cigarette makes me want to puke." They both laughed and then stopped abruptly and stared at each other.

"You don't think..."

"No, no way. I didn't do anything to..." She touched her belly.

She heard Jacob's voice in her head, "I just want to rest and go to where I am supposed to be. Help me sister, help me." Visions of *Rosemary's Baby* flashed through her mind. He would never do that to me; she decided - too many horror movies.

Doctor Ray came in at that awkward moment and cleared his throat. "Okay, all is in order, what can I do to help?"

Chapter Twenty Two
Harmon Springs
2000

Her will is strong,
So strong even in death
If he had lived...
If he had survived...

They parked on the road that ran alongside the country cemetery. Dr. Ray took the story in stride. Angie was watching his reaction as they told the doctor the story from the moment of the phone call she made from the restaurant. He nodded at places. He asked a few questions in others. He didn't make any real comments other than to give some general directions to the cemetery.

As a group, they decided to check things out at the cemetery first; they needed to verify the information before going to the sheriff's office. They walked along the headstones quietly. The doctor commented on a few of the families.

"Angie, you might be interested in this family, they are a distant branch of the Mason's, on your dad's side." He was instantly uncomfortable once he said it, after what they had just told him about Ken Mason. It was unusual to think of the man in a negative light. The mayor was known for his fairness in dealing with the politics of the town. He was known to be a bit moody, but everyone knew he loved Harmon Springs. The doctor's confidence in his beloved town was shaken.

Angie looked down at the large family stone. She felt thankful that the doctor didn't seem to pass any judgment about her father. Maybe he had seen worse in his lifetime, or maybe it was just his bedside manner, but she smiled up at him, thankful for him. They moved on.

"Let me see that chicken scratch map."

Angie handed Dr. Ray the map she had drawn hastily from Jacob's directions. He held the map at arm's length, studied it for a minute, looked up, and headed deeper into the graveyard. He followed it right to the grave. "Yes, it's correct. This is old Mrs. Jessup's grave. Interesting. And neither of you have ever been here?"

"No, I did notice the cemetery when I drove by earlier, but I didn't stop and look around or anything," Angie replied.

Peter added, "I didn't even know this place existed."

"Well, this helps your story." They all stood looking at a small square stone. It simply stated, "Ethel Jessup, Born 1899 died 1963, Beloved Mother." Birds and crickets sang around them as they stood staring at the stone. Doctor Ray broke the silence, "this would be the grave we would have to unearth. Let's go talk to the sheriff." They agreed with silent nods and left the cemetery.

The sheriff's station was abuzz with townspeople. The doctor walked in first. "Oh, Dr. Ray, I'm so glad to see you," the sheriff's secretary came up to him immediately.

"Hey, Jessica, how's your day?

The secretary walked with him to a quiet corner behind the counter. They whispered for a moment. Angie and Peter watched them. Angie was watching, hoping they weren't going to be arrested for trespassing on the spot. Peter was watching the secretary, feeling smug, hoping that she remembered how rude she had been to him not too long ago. They watched the doctor and secretary exchange a few words. He took her hands and seemed to be saying something reassuring. They watched the doctor break from her with a concerned look as he walked back to join them. He led them out of the building.

He stood facing them.

"Okay, Doc," Peter ventured, "break it to us gently." Angie nodded. Dr. Ray cleared his throat.

"This is what they know for sure. The Sheriff's car is sitting by a large lake not far from the sanatorium. There was a type of suicide note that Jessica says was written in his handwriting. She said the note mentioned something about 'sins of the father' and that he could not live with the guilt anymore." Dr. Ray dabbed his eyes. "I just can't believe it. I delivered him. I watched him grow up. It's not like him. Now his father was another story. He was moody and secretive. But not his boy. They think he is in the lake; some farmers are there now checking it out."

"I am so sorry." Angie put her hand on his arm. Doctor Ray patted her hand.

"Thank you. I just don't know what to think. They are looking into it. I just don't know where we go from here. If the sheriff isn't available, then who do we ask?"

"Is there a judge, or someone we can get permission to dig up the Jessup lady from?" Peter asked.

The doctor scratched his head. "I don't know. Judge Aiken may be in. He would be the one to give us permission. I don't know if I can help you anymore. I need some time to help my people here. Can you go get a room and call me in a couple of hours?

"Yes, of course. We will call your office in a bit. Thanks so much for your help." Angie nudged Peter.

"Oh, and yes, thanks for the..." he touched his head.

The doctor smiled and turned to go help his people.

Chapter Twenty Three
Harmon Springs
2000

The dark road called to him
He couldn't remember why he was there
The fog in his mind,
Inspired by spirits
Dulled his vision.
He swerved...

"Angie, this is crazy. It's dark out here. How are we going to do this? This is breaking the law." Peter angrily lugged the shovel as they moved through the headstones.

"I can't help it. We have to do this now. We don't have time to deal with miles of red tape and small-town bureaucracy."

"Well, I hope you think we will have time to do time. I wonder what the sentence is for grave robbing is these days." He muttered.

"Here it is. Let's just do this. If we just find his body, it will prove our story."

"And then what? This is crazy."

"Quit saying that!" Angie grumbled, "I don't know. I'm making this up as I go."

"Yeah, I can tell."

"Just help me dig." She broke the ground first. After an hour and a half, they hit something solid. They both looked at each other, dirty-faced and exhausted.

"Angie?"

"Yeah?"

"When is the last time you had a cigarette?"

She laughed. "You know, I don't know. I still don't even want one. I can't remember the last time I smoked, and I really can't remember the last time I've gone this long without smoking. Hell, I would have liked to smoke in my sleep if I could get away with it. Weird. Why?"

"I just noticed that you've been walking and digging without wheezing and coughing."

"Yup. Are you ready for this?"

"Yeah. Let's do this."

They dug around the hard vault. "We are going to have to pry this open, and the casket will be inside. This is so crazy. You know that?" He wiped the sweat from his forehead.

Angie nodded, "yes, I know."

They pried open the cement chamber. The casket inside was in perfect condition. They both looked at the smooth surface that reflected the light of the quarter moon above. Together they grabbed the sides of the casket and opened it.

"Hand me the flashlight." Angie ordered. Peter handed it to her; she noted his shaking hand. She shined the light down at the occupant. Laying there in a fit of dust and ruffles was the molded skeleton of an older woman. "Okay, he should be in the folds of her dress." She said, steeling herself up for reaching down into the dead woman's skirts.

"Be careful, Angie."

"Really? What is she going to do? Rise up and bite my neck? Geez."

"Oh, the sarcasm."

She was feeling around the skirts and stopped. She whispered. "There is something here." Angie pulled something from the skirts. A small bundle wrapped in dry rotted cloths. She awkwardly climbed out of the hole, holding the small bundle. Angie placed it carefully on the ground. They both looked down at it.

"Well," Peter asked.

"God, this is so awful." She reached down to unwrap the small package.

"Wait!" Dr. Ray came running with someone next to him. "Wait, don't touch anything." The two older men, gasping for breath, stopped just short of the small wrapped bundle. The doctor grabbed his knees. "They haven't found the sheriff yet. This is the Judge. Let's try to make this as legal as possible."

They all looked down at the small, tightly wound bundle. The Judge moved forward, leaned down, and gingerly began to unwrap it. After unraveling impossible amounts of decaying cloth, a small skeleton was exposed. Impossibly small.

"This was in the coffin?" the Judge asked.

"Yes, sir." It was Peter who answered. He wasn't looking at the Judge, or the baby, but at Angie. She was staring down at the child. She was sobbing.

"He was so small, so defenseless, so innocent." She hid her face in Peter's arm. He reached around and held her while she cried.

Dr. Ray turned to the Judge. "Do you think it's him?"

The Judge scratched his nine o'clock beard. "Well, the time is right; it seems like it would fit. Was there anything else in the casket?"

Angie sobbed, "I don't know, I stopped when I found him." She wiped her eyes and nose and said, "I hope I didn't disturb anything. I am so sorry. I just…"

The Judge looked concerned about Angie. "Okay, I'm just going to take a look. Dr. Ray, can you help me get my old bones down in that hole?"

"Yes, sir."

They moved over to the hole, and the Judge crawled down. They could hear him talking to Mrs. Jessup. "I am so sorry to disturb you Grandma. I'm trying to help you out here."

Angie and Peter looked at each other.

"Doctor, can you shine that light down here?" Dr. Ray did, and they all saw what the Judge saw. Also hidden in the folds was a small book.

"What is that?" Angie asked.

"It's a diary or a journal," the Judge answered, "and it ain't my Grandmothers. I can tell you that for sure. She couldn't read or write. Help me up, Doc."

They gathered around to look at the small ratty volume. Dr. Ray held the flashlight. The Judge opened the book and as he did, it started to disintegrate from mold and rot.

The Judge turned to the inside cover. The name 'Clyde Harrison' was written there in plain block letters. Everyone looked at Angie. She looked up in astonishment.

"And the plot thickens." Peter broke the silence. Everyone chuckled uncomfortably.

"So, does this mean it was Clyde Harrison who killed the baby boy? But why? What would possess him?" the Judge scratched his head.

Dr. Ray added, "If he did, that means that Annabelle Mason did not murder her baby. She was institutionalized unfairly because she was innocent. We took her life." He shook his head.

"There is no way we could have known the truth, Doc. We did what we thought was right." The Judge put his hand on Dr. Ray's shoulder.

Peter broke in. "I don't mean to sound crazy, being that we are all standing in the middle of a cemetery, huddled around a dead baby, in the dark of night, but we did find out a few things at Iron Rope." He had the attention of the group. "We found out that Jacob just wanted to protect Angie and that he wanted his body to be found."

The Judge cocked his head. "So, you mean to tell me that we are all here because of information you found out from Jacob?" As he said his name, he pointed down at the decayed skeleton. "So, you were talkin' to a ghost and a ghost told you that?"

Peter turned defensive. "What? Me telling you what a 'ghost' said is freakier than digging up a murdered baby in the middle of the night?"

"Well," Dr. Ray conceded, "you might have something there. This story has been a big part of this town's history. Angie here, our lost Angela, is back, and now we know what happened. So, now what?"

Angie spoke up, though she didn't even know she was going to speak or what she was going to say. "Now we make it right. I will write an article for the local paper. You do have a local paper, correct?" Both the Judge and the Doctor nodded. "Good. I will write his story and then we will bury Jacob properly, next to his mother. He knows where she is buried on the sanatorium grounds. We will mark her grave, and his. Then he will be able to rest. We also need to identify and have proper burials for all the souls buried on that property."

"Well, that sounds all well and good, but I just don't think it's going to be that easy." The voice speaking came from the tree line. A shadow moved towards them. Angie had the uncomfortable realization that she wasn't armed in any way, other than the shovel. The group stared at the approaching man. It was the Sheriff.

The Judge let out an audible sigh. "Oh my God, we thought you was a gonner. What the hell you doin' sneakin' up on us like that?" The Judge shinned the light at the Sheriff, and quickly realized his mistake. The group all gasped at the same time. It wasn't the current Sheriff. It was Clyde Harrison, dead now for many years. His face was a twisted horror, and his eyes were completely black.

Sherriff Clyde Harrison tipped his hat at Angie and said, "Sorry, Judge, I didn't mean to startle you." He looked amused. "What you all ain't ever seen a ghost?" He laughed. Then he stopped abruptly. "Put him back."

The Judge and the Doctor exchanged quick glances.

The old sheriff appeared next to Angie's ear. "You are next." He then reappeared in front of the group and pointed at them. "Now you will put that body back in that grave, along with the book, and rebury them. I told my boy to do it right and he didn't. I had to fix him. He was weak. The baby stays buried. Our secrets stay buried."

"What's the big deal? You are dead. Why do you care?" Doctor Ray questioned him.

The Sheriff looked confused. "It's all there in the diary; I know you all read it. I was in love with Clarisse and had been since we was young. I didn't want my wife finding that out. It woulda killed her." He stood looking from confused face to confused face.

Angie reached down and picked up her dead baby brother. She held him as if he still lived. She looked at the Sheriff. "You loved my Grandmother. All he wanted to do was protect her from pain and suffering." With her other hand, she tossed the worn journal at the Sheriff. "There is nothing left of the journal. You shouldn't have killed Jacob, but you did. This is your sin to bear. Let us bury Jacob by our mother. He has been holding your town hostage in anger and vengeance. This is how to revitalize this town. I know that deep down you are a good man. People loved you and respected you. You can do the right thing here."

He was standing defiantly with a gun pointed at them but he was slowing, losing strength. He looked over at Peter, "Why do you look so damn familiar?"

Peter shrugged. "My mother was a drug addict from a couple towns over. She was a prostitute like her mother before her. I am Angie's cousin. Annabelle and my mom were sisters, but they never knew each other existed."

"How do you know that?" the Sheriff asked in shock.

Angie picked up the story. "Jacob told us. He said that it was time that the sins of the father needed to be paid for. You and the mayor,

Ken Mason, took advantage of a young girl and that young girl produced twins. You didn't know there were twins. You took one and gave it to Ken and his wife, but you didn't tell Ken it was his real daughter. So, when Ken took advantage of her later, he had no idea what an even greater tragic mistake he was making. That young woman, her name was Janelle, by the way, raised her other daughter.

"Janelle, my Grandmother," Peter added, "became a prostitute and drug addict, and so her daughter followed suit. When her daughter was 16, she delivered me. My life was horrible until the State came and rescued me. What is really weird is that I met Angie years later, in college up in Chicago, miles and miles away from here. It's like our paths just had to cross."

Angie put her arm around him and hugged him. The men didn't move. There was an uncomfortable silence filled with confusion.

Angie stepped closer to the apparition and held out her dead brother. "Make this right. Let this town go. Aren't you tired?"

The old Sheriff looked at the remains of the baby and his ethereal body became thinner.

A blinding light opened up next to the old Sheriff. A younger version of him reached out to pull him through. Everyone but Angie gasped in recognition of the younger Sheriff pulling his father into the light. The light became too bright, and group shielded their eyes. The cemetery shivered. The light disappeared and where the old Sheriff stood there was a black void. It radiated evil and had the shape of a young woman for only a moment. Then it disappeared.

Angie spoke first. "Who was that?"

"That young man was our Sheriff, Clyde's son," the Judge answered slowly. "God rest his soul. I don't know who that woman was."

Dr. Ray walked over to the place where the apparitions were. He kneeled, touching the hallowed ground. "It was some concentrated evil. I can still feel it."

The group agreed with silent nods.

Peter asked, "Was that Annabelle?"

"No. I could only see her outline, but I would know Annabelle if I saw her." Dr. Ray stood and walked over to Jacob and took his body from Angie's arms.

"Maybe it was her mother," Angie whispered as she let the Doctor take her brother.

"Maybe. Let's get back into town." Dr. Ray and the Judge worked to shut the coffin and close the vault. "We'll come back in the morning and restore Mrs. Jessup back to her resting place. Let's get out of the cemetery.

The evening cricket songs resumed their symphonies.

Chapter Twenty Four
Harmon Springs
1999

Drink the sweet tea
And pour the strong coffee
Make all the food fresh and local
Share memories and accomplishments
Hold each other close because
That is all we have

Clarisse turned on her bedside lamp. The lamp only gave a token of light. It was after midnight. She propped herself up on her elbows, wondering what woke her up. She listened and heard nothing. She clicked the light off and focused on the evening glow coming in through her window. Her eyelids began to close, and then she heard it again. A whisper.

"Grandmother."

She kept her eyes closed and stayed still. *It's my mind playing tricks on me.*

"Grandmother."

"Who is there," she answered, thinking of where her long-dead husband's gun was. She sat up and snapped the light back on. At that moment, she realized that her husband's gun was not going to work on the voice. She knew who it was, though she didn't understand how it could be. Only one male child's voice could call her grandmother.

"Yes, Grandmother. You are right. I've come to help you. I've come to deliver you from your pain."

Tears of confused joy and fear streamed as she looked around, though knowing it was impossible that her grandson could be in the room. She felt a cold little hand press on her mouth and her nose. *My grandson.*

The boy stepped back and looked at the now lifeless body. "Goodbye, Grandmother. You were loved. You were innocent and a victim. You have suffered enough." The boy shimmered back into nothing.

Chapter Twenty Five
Harmon Springs
2000

The sweet spring wind
Wrapped around them
Butterflies sang
Joyously
All was right, all was good
Even the quiet one settled
Into the last happy moment,
Accepting his fate.

Peter knocked on the door of the large Southern Antebellum Plantation home. The porch fit his imagination of what an old plantation home would look like. It made him happy to think of Angie living there. So much had happened in this town. So many skeletons, not just hiding in the closets, but busting out of the rafters and filling up the town with secrets and hidden anger. He was holding a bottle of white wine, a moving in gift for the dinner that Angie was preparing. She opened the door and laughed.

"Peter! You don't have to knock! Please! We're relatives. *Mi casa es tu casa!*" She took his bottle and hugged him tight.

"Ohhh hey, I can't breathe," he laughed as they walked arm and arm down the hallway towards the kitchen. "Damn, girl. This is nice! Now you need a big ole family to fill it up!"

She put the bottle on ice. "I don't want any kids for a long time. That was a scare for a bit there. All that crazy stuff happening, I was just thinking it would be just my luck to get pregnant from some malignant spirit."

"Yeah, especially weird because he was bad, and your brother, and a baby. That is weird."

"Well, weird, but it was good to finally get some answers."

Peter laughed, "I think you've earned a new nickname, 'ghost buster' or something."

"A new nickname? I wasn't aware that I had one in the first place." She grabbed the deep-dish soup tureen.

"Umm yeah. Dragon Queen of the restaurant business." He gathered the dinner plates and they walked to the dining room.

"I wasn't that bad. I only got that nickname because I liked to eat at that Chinese Dragon restaurant. The name stuck. So how is the firm doing without you?"

He shrugged and rearranged a napkin.

She stopped filling their wine glasses. "You did tell them you weren't coming back. Right?"

"Yes, silly." He sat down. "This looks great." He placed his napkin in his lap. She sat across from him.

"Thank you, sir!" she placed her napkin in her lap also. "I have been so looking forward to chicken and dumplings. Thanks for coming over."

"No problem. Thanks for giving me the night off so I could eat with you, boss lady." He smiled good-naturedly as he took his first bite. "Wow," he said between bites, "why is this so good?"

She smiled her all-knowing smile. "You know I can't give away any secrets. I will tell you, though, that I found this recipe in Grandma's recipe book. I'm sure that makes it extra tasty. That and the free-range chicken that was on sale at the farmer's market."

"It's amazing. Let's add it to the menu for Sundays. Can we?"

"Sure." She acknowledged with a bite in her mouth. He smiled. They finished their bowls and mopped up the thick chicken broth with the homemade rolls.

He pushed his bowl away and remembered his wine. He sipped and placed it back on the table. "So, how are you doing here? Does it feel awkward?"

She considered for a moment, "No, it's good. It makes me sad. It's like I can see the life I missed. I walk through the rooms and I see pictures of holiday gatherings, my mother, my father, and so much more. You should see the attic! Maybe we can go up there later. It's like a museum. And Annabelle's room is still here like she is going to walk into it at any moment. It's comforting to sit in there, on her bed. I keep wondering what it was like for her here."

"Has Dr. Ray added anything to what you already knew about her?"

"No, not really. He just examined her on the day they committed her. I need to take her medical records over to him and let him look at them. He might be able to find some hidden doctor lingo in it."

"I didn't realize there were parts that needed to be figured out."

"Some parts are kind of...cryptic. Maybe it's nothing, who knows. You know, I still haven't had any blackouts or any weirdness since we've arrived here." She knocked on the thick oak table.

"Angie, that's amazing. You think it could be because you are where you are supposed to be?"

"I don't know. I know I don't want to question it too much, but I also don't want to put it so far back on the 'to do' list that I totally forget about it, you know?" She sipped and smiled at Peter.

"What? Do I have something in my teeth?" he instinctively started to wrestle with a toothpick from the container on the table.

"No, silly. Grab your drink and let's explore upstairs." Like two kids, they scampered upstairs and then pulled down the ladder to climb into the attic.

"I'll go first; I've been up there once. The light is right at the top." They stood in a dusty, dimly-lit attic that spanned the five thousand square foot southern home. The lights were rigged to run the gamut of the space, but they didn't give off much light. Angie wondered when the last time they had been changed. Maybe the light bulbs themselves were antiques.

Peter whistled. "Wow, this is ... I don't know what this is."

"It's a museum that looks like it was run by a crazy person. A totally crazy person."

Old, threads of spider webs were everywhere. Some items were covered with cloths; some were bare and staring at them with cold eyes. Toys. The attic was full of toys.

Peter whispered as he carefully wiped a thick layer of oily dust off of a rocking horse, "Hey, isn't this the title of an old bestselling novel, *Toys in the Attic*?"

"No," she whispered back, "That's *Flowers in the Attic*."

"Oh. Why are we whispering?"

"I don't know," she whispered back.

They stepped over broken toys and boxes of baby clothes. Angie picked her way toward the south wall. She had spied the chifferobe when she checked out the attic with the electrician. She had to climb a bit and maneuver over piles of baby dolls, all of which were watching her. She felt like they were judging her. Is she a good witch or a bad one? She giggled.

"Angie. I heard a giggle. Oh, my God. He's back." Peter hissed.

"It was me, you big silly."

Peter harrumphed, and they continued exploring.

Angie moved boxes of old, odd objects to get closer to the dresser. Once she cleared away the boxes, she stood in front of the chifferobe. She opened the top door. Inside were, of course, more boxes, but smaller ones. She picked one up and opened it. *Pandora.* That's what she felt like. Inside the box, there were little bits of paper. She unfolded one. It was a poem. Okay, she thought to herself. Maybe not Pandora, maybe more Emily Dickinson.

> Poem 453
> The clouds are black and blue,
> Sadly looking
> Down at all of us
> Wondering why we shuffle,
> We struggle,
> They move on,
> No longer concerned with
> Human happenings.
> The nightly noises of those left behind
> Lull the ghosts to sleep.

She refolded the paper carefully and opened another one.

> Poem 991
> He will hate you
> Make your life crazy
> Willis hates everyone
> His will is made of iron
> His feelings made of lead.
> Stay away.

She carefully folded it and opened another. Peter made her jump. "Hey, what did you find?" He was looking over her shoulder.

"It's poetry. It's prophetic poetry."

"What is that? Like Nostradamus? I didn't think that was poetry, I thought..."

"No, not like that. This is like random little poems about my life and your life. See, look at this." She handed him Poem 991. He read it and handed it back.

"It's cryptic. I don't get it. But I never do get poetry."

"It seems cryptic to you, but to me it makes perfect sense. Willis is the last name of that annoying neighbor I had. Remember I told you about him? He was leaving threatening notes on my door complaining about the noise. But the noise couldn't have been me because I was never home. "

"But how can that be true? I mean how can it be written on that piece of paper? This has got to be decades old." He flipped the paper over. It was heavy and unlined.

"I don't know. Help me grab these boxes. I need some better light." They gathered up armfuls of boxes and hauled them down the ladder.

They started to spread them over the large antique dining room table.

They opened up the little folded slips of paper and spread them on the table. It was a world of poems, words that swirled together, telling a story that would be hard to believe.

"They are so beautiful." Angie sat and contemplated them. "I think they are my mom's."

Peter sat down also. "Why?"

"Look at the details." She picked one up. "Like this one, number 701..."

Poem 701
The pain hurts him and drives him
To hurt others.
The pain hurts him
And he lashes out
He just wants to be free
Free from the skirts
Of her death embrace.

"That's Jacob. Buried in that grave with that woman. I got that. Man. That is crazy. I don't guess there's one in there about me winning the lottery?" Peter started reading through them faster.

"I don't think so, at least not yet. But just wrap your mind around this. If this is Annabelle's poetry, or whatever it is, then she knew everything. She knew everything that was going to happen. She knew about stuff that happened to me just last year. That means she knew we would meet...that Jacob would kill people, that she would be committed, that she would get a lobotomy; she knew everything."

"So, she wasn't mentally challenged. She was psychic or something?"

"I guess, let's try to put these in some sort of order."

"Okay, but I don't think they will fit on the table."

"You're right. Let's line them up in the great room. There is a lot of floor space there."

The great room was one of the best rooms in the house except, of course, the kitchen. The floors were mahogany, old, sturdy, and well-loved. The fireplace took up most of one wall. The large floor to ceiling windows, though not a real southern style feature, were perfect for natural light. The view was a perfect balance of woods and the garden.

They laid out the slips of paper on the floor and started the long process of putting the puzzle together. It was a tedious process.

"Let's just put the ones we don't understand in a pile over here."

"Okay, but look at this one..." he handed it to Angie.

Poem 2
And then it was good,
This day
This day of fun
And play
When the sun is warm
And the children sing
And

"And what?"

"That is it." She handed the slip to Peter. "And look at that number. There are so many, and this one isn't finished."

"Just keep it separate. If we find anymore that aren't done, we will bunch them together."

Hours later, the floor was covered with neat lines of little slips of paper. The numbers didn't match up, but they were all in some sort of chronological order. Then there was the pile that they didn't know what to do with.

Peter broke the silence as they looked in wonder at the story they just lived through, and their relatives just lived through. "The numbers mean something. I know there's a pattern."

Angie picked one up. "It's not chronological. This is number 4 and it is here near the end, next to number 499."

"Maybe it has something to do with who the poem is about?"

"But what about the poems that are about more than one person?" she asked.

"True. This really triggers my OCD. I know there's a pattern. I have a crazy idea." He went to the foyer and grabbed his laptop bag. He walked into the great room triumphantly. "I am going to log these in. Then once they are logged in, I can move them around and find the pattern."

"So, you are spending the night?" she asked, amused.

"Sweetie, it's already two a.m. I think I'm here for the night."

"Wow, where did the time go? Okay, you type and I'll dictate."

They worked diligently through the night. The first morning birds sang, and Angie snapped awake. "Oh no, how long have I been asleep?"

Peter didn't answer because he was fast asleep next to his laptop. She smiled and reached over and shook him awake.

"Oh, I fell asleep, sorry."

"I did too. Did we finish?"

Peter turned his computer back on. He looked for a moment. "Angie. I think I see the pattern."

"Let's have it, Rain Man."

"Look here, see how these numbers run? What was that? Were you expecting someone?" he asked as the doorbell sounded.

"No, not this early for sure. Hang on; I'll go see who it is." Angie walked quickly to the front part of the house.

She opened the door. Redd stood on her porch with a small box in his hands.

"Oh, hey, Redd, what brings you by so early?" Angie opened the door to let him in.

"Well, I just found this and I thought you might be interested in it. Wow, what are you guys up to?" Piles of papers were lined up all over the great room's floor.

Peter answered, yawning, "We found these 'poems' in the attic, and we've been trying to put them in some sort of order."

Redd sat in an overstuffed antique armchair. "Well, looks like I got here at the right time." He opened the box and inside was a bound notebook. He handed it to Angie. "This is for you. I had forgotten all about it. Clarisse gave it to me years ago, saying that I might need to give it away some time in the future. I asked her what she meant, but she said to trust her, and I did. I don't know why I thought about it this mornin'. I just had to bring it over when I remembered."

"What is it, Redd?" Angel stood holding the notebook.

"I think it's what you're lookin' for."

Angie opened the notebook. It was the same handwriting on the slips of paper. Each page held a group of numbers and on each page a list of names and events and dates filled in the lines. She looked up at Peter, who was watching her expectantly. "It's a key. It's the pattern."

Chapter Twenty Six
Harmon Springs
2001

Is it death, or is it birth
That makes us question
Why it happens
The way it does
The good die.
The bad die.
The rain falls on the just
And unjust alike.
The only constant is change,
Hold onto it,
Embrace it.

"Hey, Redd!" Angie greeted him happily as she cleaned the counter, where she knew he would sit.

"Well, good morning, Angie! So nice to see your smiling face! How was business last night?" He sat at the counter in his honorary spot. She poured his coffee without his having to ask.

"It was great. I think we are going to need to hire a server and a cook to keep up with the tourists and town business." She smiled and showed him the P and L account book. He grinned at the profit margin.

"I am just amazed. Angie, our town is reborn. How are you doing staying in your grandma's home? Everything okay?"

"Yes, it's warm and comforting. Every day I find something new that she tucked away. I found a baby picture of me and Jacob and a whole box of photos of my mother. She was so beautiful. I feel so bad for all she had to go through. Did Grandma ever mention why she didn't visit Annabelle? Why didn't she claim her when she died?"

Redd sipped his coffee. Angie poured herself a cup. "Well, I was wonderin' if you were ever gonna ask. I was thinkin' I would bring it up to save you the trouble. I don't know much 'cause she didn't share much. We knew it hurt her to talk about Annabelle or about you, but there were times that she seemed to be in the sharin' mood. We all loved Mrs. Clarisse, so you have to know we never judged her, and we never pushed her."

"I understand, Redd. I just didn't know if you knew anything about it."

"Well, lemme think. It was about six years ago. I remember because it was the town's centennial. The whole town just about showed up to celebrate in the town square. The town was already sparsely populated.

Redd's story played on the countertop like a clip from a made-for-TV movie.

-1995-

Clarisse sat on the bench outside her cafe. She had the best view of the festivities. Her eyes were tired. Tired of the hurt; the meanness of life. Maybe even the meaninglessness of it. She watched the older couples dancing in the city square. It was alarming how there were fewer and fewer young people in their town. Any young people that were born here left as soon as humanly possible, and many times whole families moved out. Harmon Springs was dying a slow, sad death. The bell on her door rang and Redd stepped out into the twilight air.

"Hey, Redd." She didn't want to startle him.

"Oh, hey, Mrs. Clarisse! I didn't notice you sitting there. Ain't it a beautiful night?"

"Oh, yes. It is. Redd sit here with me a bit, will you?"

"Why yes, I would love to!" Redd sat next to Clarisse and they both sat quietly watching the fun."

"Redd. When your wife died, did you feel like she was still hanging around, like you could hear her sometimes? Maybe see her out of the corner of your eye?"

Redd chuckled, "Well now, I ain't saying I ever saw no ghost, but I do feel like sometimes she's a lookin' down on me. Are you worryin' about something? Sometimes our minds plays tricks on us when we worry too much."

"Maybe I am. Business is slow, but I'm not hurting for money. When Ken died, well, he made sure I was taken care of. But I swear sometimes, I think I just...oh, I don't' know. I sound crazy, don't I?"

"Aw, no, we all know how hard life is. Heck, I think we all have a little crazy in us to stay livin' here."

"I wanted to go see her." She said the statement flatly, not making eye contact. He didn't need to ask who she was talking about. "I hated not claiming her when she died. It was wrong. I'm going to go to hell for sure."

"Now, you don't go beatin' yourself up. They didn't notify you that she died until they done buried her, so there was nothin' you could do about that," he reassured her.

"I should have gone to visit her. If I had, they would have known she had family that cared."

"Life is full of shoulda's and coulda's. We can't help what happens that is outta our control."

"I did love her and Angela. I did. I know it's cliché, but part of me died when they went away. I never forgave Ken when he sent them away. I begged him not to. He wouldn't hear of it. It was out of my control." A tear rolled down her deeply wrinkled face. "I should have fought him harder."

"No, you couldn't have done that. You know you couldn't do that."

She swallowed the lump in her throat. "I wish I could find Angela. If I could just see her and maybe just hold her; spoil her just like a grandmother should."

"It'll be okay; you never know. Maybe they will come back to visit kinfolk or something."

"Maybe." She looked up again at the party in the street. "Let's go join them."

"It would be my pleasure!" He stood and offered his chunky calloused hand. She took it gratefully and they walked towards the square.

-2001-

"She didn't mention it again. We danced a little and visited with neighbors and she went on home, I went on home, and the days were the same from then on out. She worked in the café; I became the best regular, if I don't say so myself." He smiled as Angie refilled his coffee. "I can tell you that she was real sad. She would laugh once in a while, but it was rare. She only found peace when she was working here. She tried to stay on at the school, but it was just too much stress on her, and she said once that she couldn't handle seeing the young girls because she thought she saw Annabelle around every corner."

"I wish I would have come just a few months sooner. I would have gotten to meet her."

"I know she would have loved that. She was old, heck, we are all gettin' older, but she still had her sense about her. Her arthritis was real bad, and she couldn't work at all. But her mind was as sharp as ever." He smiled deep in memories of his old friend. "She would have loved to meet you. All she ever wanted to do was spoil you. I bet she is lookin' down from heaven so proud of you, takin' over the place. This was her second dream, takin' care of you and Annabelle was her first."

"Didn't she love...errr...her husband?" It was still difficult to admit he was her father.

He hesitated and stared at his coffee. "In those days, you married for better or for worse. I think theirs was for the worst. But she stood by him, though; I think if she had known...if she had known the truth, she would have walked away. I'm sure of it."

"Well, I need to get ready for the breakfast crowd. Redd, as co-owner of Annabelle's, will you do the honors of turning on the open sign?" She smiled sweetly.

"It would be my pleasure!" He got up and switched on the sign. Customers rolled in at a leisurely pace and the day moved in loving grace.

Later that evening she turned her apron over to her trusted friend Peter for the night shift. It didn't take much to convince him to stay in Harmon Springs. He was also a co-owner of Annabelle's Cafe and a professional blogger about southern cuisine and culture. It wasn't what he went to school for, but it didn't matter. The town accepted him with open arms. They did not care about his flamboyant ways or alternative lifestyle. They loved him as a son and he loved them back.

Angie smiled as she walked along to the local cemetery. It had been a year now since the night they dug up her brother's body. She walked through the cemetery to put flowers on the graves of the only family she cared about.

Later, after the funeral and the initial shock of her returning to town, she visited the doctor again. She walked back into that now familiar clinic. The admitting nurse, Missy (they were on a first-name basis now), smiled at her. "Hello there, Angie, what can we do for you today?"

"Is Dr. Ray in?"

"Yes, he is. Are you just visiting or do you need him for medical reasons?"

Good question. "Just stopping by to say hi. Is he in his office?"

"Yes, you can go on back. I don't think he will mind." Angie hoped not. He took her under his wing after that fateful night. She knew he was paying for whatever he felt he had done wrong, but she was still grateful for him stepping up and even believing their incredible story. She peeked into his office; he was writing something, deep in thought.

"Hey Dr. Ray," she said softly.

He looked up and smiled a genuine smile. "Hello, Angie! What brings you by today? I was just thinking about you. Have a seat! And I think you can call me Shaun. We've been through a lot. I think we are friends enough now."

Angie smiled and sat down. "So, how are things?"

"Fabulous! I delivered two babies last week. That was great. Now I'm working on a proposal to add on to the clinic because families are moving back to town, not to mention the influx of tourists. You have to be ready for that kind of thing. People fall, they get hurt, sick, they need medical care." He smiled. "Times are changing for the better. I know you had to go through a lot of hard times and scary times, but you have to know that our town is so much better because of you."

Angie blushed. "Oh, I don't know about all that. But I'm so excited and happy to finally have a place to fit in. Of course, the restaurant corporation world was sad to lose me, but they understood."

"Good, good. And what about Annabelle's Cafe? Was the takeover peaceful?"

It was a bit of a surprise to everyone that Clarisse had left Annabelle's to Angela if she ever returned to the town to claim anything.

"I bet she thought that if I did claim her inheritance that I would do so and cash it in and leave town as fast as possible."

"Oh, I don't know. I think she had hopes that you would come back and live here again. I was surprised that she left you everything, the house, and the cafe. I know I'm glad you decided to stay. So, what can I help you with? I see that determined look in your face."

"I need a favor, but a secret one."

He looked concerned.

"It's not that bad, don't worry." She pulled a paper out of her bag. "I was wondering if you would like to be a co-owner of Annabelle's Cafe." She watched his reaction carefully. Surprise and interest. Good. "I know it's not your usual line of business, but you can be sure that it won't be a huge leap of financial faith. I'm dividing up the ownership between myself, you, Peter, and Redd." He closed his file folder and sat back. Something was churning behind his eyes. She let him digest and process for a minute. "What do you think? You don't have to answer right now; you can think about it."

Dr. Ray leaned forward with a very serious look. "I don't need to think about it. I'm in. If we want to revitalize this town, we need to invest in it. I'm proud and honored that you are asking me to be a part of Annabelle's Cafe. Now I have to ask a favor of you."

Angie was ecstatic. "Oh, sure! Anything."

He closed his eyes. "I want to tell you why I helped you that night."

"You do not have to do that. I am so grateful for all you've done. Whatever your reasons were, it doesn't matter now. You have done your part to set things right; at least, I believe you have."

"Exactly, I need to tell you this, for my own conscience. I helped you all that night because I needed to. It was me who helped to commit Annabelle."

"It's okay really. You were just doing what you thought was right. I don't..."

"No, hear me out. I was just out of medical school, and I wanted to be accepted into the town. Yes, I had opened my practice, and yes, I selected this town over the hundreds of others that needed doctors. I felt drawn to this place. So, my first year as a doctor, I spent here. The town's folk were happy to have me. Because I opened a practice, they didn't have to go to Iron Rope or to some other place to receive medical care.

"Your Grandfather, err, Father, God what a horrible man, came to me in a panic. I was eager to help him because, though the town was happy to have me, I was a newcomer, and I didn't feel like I was as trusted as I needed to be. He was frantic and desperate. He said that his daughter killed her newborn baby and that she was 'feeble-minded' and was there any way he could have her committed. He couldn't bear to see her go to jail. I told him that, of course, he could have her committed; it was just a matter of signing some paperwork. Back in those days, any man could commit any woman just on his word, whether she needed mental care or not. It was a sad state of affairs.

"So, with my signature and his, we committed Annabelle Mason. I had never examined her, other than that day they brought her in. I just committed her on his word and then moved on with life. From that day, I've been heavy with guilt. I never married. I never had children. I never had the clichéd happiness of the American dream. I haven't regretted that choice. I was drawn to this town to serve a purpose. I thought my purpose was to help heal the sick, but then I began to notice the sick in this town were not sick from physical ailments. There was something darker, lurking. So, when you showed up with your fantastic tale, I saw it as an opportunity to set something right."

"Do you think my mother was crazy? You know, lunatic asylum crazy?"

"No. I absolutely do not. Back then, you did what the husband or father wanted, especially if he was the head of the town. I only talked to her once; I didn't even deliver her children. When she delivered, a midwife was called. Your father did not want me there, and now I think I know why."

Angie nodded. "Yes, he probably hoped she would die in childbirth, or maybe we would. But he didn't know we would be a 'we'."

"True, but I also think he wanted as much privacy as possible. Annabelle was known for her eccentric behavior, so if she did die in childbirth, or her children died, he probably thought no one would think twice about it."

"But you did talk to her once?" she asked.

"Yes, it was the day I signed the paperwork to commit her. The sheriff brought her by my office and sat her in a room. He explained that she was in his custody because she killed her son. Her father would be in shortly to sign her over to the state mental asylum instead of her spending time in jail. He just needed an evaluation from me and a signature.

I walked into the examining room, and she was sitting quietly on the table. Her hands were clasped together in her lap.

"Hello, Annabelle."

She didn't respond. She stared blankly at the floor. Her fingers were moving, twisting together in some sort of prayer looking formation.

"Annabelle, I need to examine you. Will you cooperate?"

She didn't answer. She sat there twisting her fingers together, and she wouldn't make eye contact.

I did the usual exam, trying to buy time to figure out what to do. So, I looked into her ears. I checked her heartbeat and her breathing. All normal. I remember that she smelled bad. The odor burned my nose.

"Annabelle. Are you in any pain?"

She sobbed, but she didn't speak.

"I want to help you but you have to talk to me. Do you understand?" She didn't respond. "Do you understand why you are here?" No response. "You are going to be committed for killing your son. Do you understand?" She looked up at me, but not at my face. She was looking at something beyond my left ear. The sorrow in her eyes spoke the only words she could manage. I don't know how else to explain that look.

I asked her, "Did you kill your baby, Annabelle?" She sobbed again and hid her face in her hands. I wanted to comfort her, so I put my hands on her shoulders. As soon as I did, she jumped up, practically knocked me over, and ran out of the examining room. I jumped back because I didn't think she had that kind of energy in her. I yelled for her to stop and for the nurse to grab her. I ran after her and stopped short at the scene by the admitting desk. There on the floor, on her knees, was Annabelle, she was screaming, crying, at the feet of her father. He looked around at the people looking at them. He was shaken, but I felt like he wasn't upset about her. It seemed like it was how he was being perceived. He seemed visibly embarrassed by her. He kicked her off of his leg.

He turned and signed the paper on the counter. I was in shock, I guess. I didn't expect all the pain, the emotional pain, and I didn't expect her father to be so emotionless about her. I didn't know what to do. The sheriff was standing there, also without emotion, holding the paperwork. I walked over to the papers and signed them. Annabelle wailed. Then the sheriff signed the paper. He gathered her up and escorted her out.

"And that was the last I saw of Annabelle Mason. I thought, at that moment, that I was doing the right thing. I have regretted that decision as soon as I made it." The doctor sighed and smiled at Angie. "But now we have made it better, so let's move on. Where do I sign? This time, I know I'm going to do some good."

Angie slid the papers over to him while contemplating his memories. Her father was an enigma that she had to realize that she would never fully understand. It made her feel ugly to think she was part of him. The only real ideal that she could latch onto that was that she also wanted to preserve Harmon Springs. The only thing is that she was going to do it the right way.

Chapter Twenty Seven
Iron Rope Sanatorium
1980s

The common room in the children's ward was chaos. The sound of children's cries, screams, moaning, agony all melded into a cacophony of pain. Some children ran in random circles, going nowhere. Some hit their heads on the hard floor or the walls or the tables or on each other. Others just lay on the floor, crying for comfort and care.

The smell was a mixture of sour dishes of food that have been sitting too long and an outhouse that was overused and never cleaned. Some children were potty-trained, but it didn't matter. Too many weren't. Too many were not able to walk to a restroom without assistance. They were skeletons; hungry for food and hungry for attention.

The Night Nurse hated coming into this room. It wasn't part of her duty. She was looking for the new head doctor and her head supervisor said he was in here. She walked briskly, trying not to make eye contact with the starving children. She heard the doctor talking to a young boy. The boy was sitting against the wall hugging his knees. He looked about six years old. He was staring ahead.

"Johnny, who were you talking to?" the doctor asked the boy.

"The boy. I told you. The boy."

"There isn't any other boy around you right now. Johnny, now tell me the truth." The doctor was firm, but he had a kindness in his voice that the nurse had not heard from a head administrator in a long time.

The young boy started to cry. "His name is Jacob and he promised to be my friend and he wants to visit me. And you scared him away." The young boy looked directly at the doctor. "Go away."

The doctor stood up and jumped when he realized the nurse was standing there beside him.

"Okay, Johnny, but I'm coming back to check on you." The doctor motioned for the nurse to follow him.

"Hello doctor, I'm so sorry to bother you, but...."

"No, it's fine. He's a relative of my wife's, and I just ..."

"You don't have to explain." They walked towards the front lobby, away from the chaos. Once they could hear each other, she turned to plead with him. "What are we going to do? There isn't enough food. We have no help; no space. We are losing more patients from infection in this place than from other illnesses."

The doctor put his hands on her shoulders. "I know. The governor knows our plight. We will have answers by the end of the week. We will need to do the best we can until then. There's nothing else we can do."

"Are they going to get us money and help, or are they going to..." she couldn't finish the sentence because of the break in her voice.

He dropped his hands to his sides. "I don't know. I don't know. But whatever it is, we can do it and get through it together."

She nodded, still unable to speak. This was her place. These were her people. It wouldn't be a problem finding another job, but her loyalty was fierce. She did not want to leave this place. She turned to start her twenty-hour shift that didn't seem like work.

Chapter Twenty Eight
Iron Rope Sanatorium
2001

She smiles at her child
The child smiles back...
But it's only a drawing,
Paper thin,
Paper thick
But yet,
She smiles

The excavation at the sanatorium took months. Most of the bodies of the patients that died at Iron Rope were all recovered and most were identified, though some had to be buried with an anonymous engraved tombstone.

Annabelle Mason was moved to the family plot in the local cemetery. Jacob was buried next to her. Angie sat comfortably between them, breathing in the clean air.

The day of the reburial was the day that the town was reborn. No highway came through, no gold mine produced new jobs, but something lifted. Old-timers in the town would swear they could tell the moment the funeral was complete. It was like the soul of the town let out a huge sigh and then started to breathe again.

Cell towers went up, and the town linked in with the rest of the world. It became a get-a-way place for couples searching for Old-World romance. Couples walked hand and hand down the coble-stone streets that were decorated in whatever season was being celebrated. They married in the one-room church; they visited quaint shops and shared coffee in small side street cafes.

The cell towers linked the town to the world, but they were still able to keep the old-world feel. The local planning committees wanted it that way. Not to stop progress, but to celebrate simplicity and to create a digital-free getaway for artists, writers, honeymooners, anyone who needed to decompress. They didn't let any superstores in or big businesses. It was all locally owned, locally produced goods.

Once Harmon Springs advertised on the internet, people came from all over to visit their farmers' markets, their craft fairs, and to eat some of the most amazing home-cooked, locally grown fresh food. It was Angie who had insisted on the special bed and breakfast just for writers. She smiled when she thought of how it stayed booked year around.

She placed the fresh flowers on three graves. She moved closer to her mother's tombstone, and she traced the sculpted angel's upturned face on the headstone. Angie had dictated what the stone said. She was proud of it.

Annabelle Mason
...And neither the angels in heaven above,
Nor the demons down under the sea,
Can ever dissever my soul from the soul
Of the beautiful Annabel Lee.
Edgar Allan Poe
Beloved mother of Angel and Jacob, we love you, always and forever
1945 – 1975

Angie whispered a quiet prayer, "Thank you, Mom. Thank you for keeping me in your heart when your world was so dim. You never forgot me, even when they tried to erase your memory. You were strong and so brave. I hope you understand Jacob now. I am so sorry that he scared you; it wasn't his intention. He was special. He knew that we were born out of a darkness that was hidden from you, and all he wanted to do was protect me. I hope that wherever you are, you can see that."

She dried her tears and stood, taking a deep breath of the fast-approaching night air. For the first time in her life, she felt like she belonged and that she was loved. She headed back to town. The Jones' invited her over for baked lasagna and Chianti. She wasn't going to pass that up.

Poem 589
Town's people rejoice
The sun shines healthy

And bright
No longer is there a fear
Of the long dark night.
She saved the soul
Of him that needed to be saved.

Chapter Twenty Nine
Iron Rope Sanatorium
2001

Her beauty, awkward,
Strength rests in her face,
As she looks for her past,
Hand on the truth
Heart enveloped in hope,
She steps through the door
The bell rings,
The lady looks,
And she is home.

The wind blew through the halls at Iron Rope. The sun was setting pleasantly behind it. The town did not have the heart to tear down the old structure. It was Angie's idea to turn it into a study for paranormal research. People came from universities all over to study the activity. Though nothing topped the day they set Jacob free. There was still plenty for researchers to ponder on and explore.

Tonight, though, it was empty of human inhabitants. No one saw the small boy scamper and skip gleefully down the hall. He stopped at a room to peek in. His favorite lady was in there singing. She saw him peeking around her door and held her arms open for him. He skipped in and climbed in her lap. She continued her song, a soft lullaby that carried on the wind. He tucked his head into her, and she caressed his arm.

Mother and son reunited years ago, but now there was no sadness, no fear, only love. The song carried through the hallways on the nighttime breeze. Annabelle had everything now. Her daughter was a beautiful success, brave and strong. Her son was frail but sweet, snuggled into her now, forever safe from the harmful acts of man.

Acknowledgments:
I would like to thank the River Bend Writing Project (no longer a thing, thanks to budget cuts) for being the inspiration for telling Annabelle's story. I had a few "beta" readers who I am so thankful for, especially here at the end. Kim Schiavone and Carol Moore, Kathy Osborne, Jennifer Martin, and all of my book club friends - your feedback was incredible. Thank you to Diane Whitehead for your editing help! Thank you also to my friends and family who have been waiting patiently for me to "do something" with my story. If you would like to contact me with questions, feedback, and or complaints, please email me at vikitam.writer@gmail.com.

www.ingramcontent.com/pod-product-compliance
Lightning Source LLC
Chambersburg PA
CBHW031146130726
47988CB00006B/2551